LEGACY

LEGACY

A PRIVATE NOVEL

KATE BRIAN

SIMON AND SCHUSTER

First published in Great Britain in 2008 by Simon and Schuster UK Ltd
A CBS COMPANY
This edition published 2009

Originally published in the USA in 2008 by Simon Pulse,
an imprint of Simon & Schuster Children's Division, New York.

   Produced by Alloy Entertainment
151 West 26th Street, New York, NY 10001

Simon & Schuster UK Ltd
1st Floor, 222 Gray's Inn Road, London WC1X 8HB

This book is a work of fiction. Names, characters, places and incidents are either
the product of the author's imagination or are used fictitiously. Any resemblance
to actual people living or dead, events or locales is entirely coincidental.

A CIP catalogue record for this book is available from the British Library.

ISBN 978-1-84738-262-7

1 3 5 7 9 10 8 6 4 2

Printed by CPI Cox & Wyman, Reading, Berkshire RG1 8EX

www.simonandschuster.co.uk

LEGACY

SHALLOW

Death.

It wasn't supposed to happen this way. The only two people I had ever known who had died had died young. Had died beautiful. Had died horrifying, gruesome deaths.

Had died because of me.

Wait. Stop. No.

Not because of me. I couldn't think that way. Not without going insane. Thomas had died because Ariana was psychotic. Cheyenne had died because she was disturbed. It was not my fault. Not mine.

So why couldn't I help thinking that if I had never come to Easton Academy, they would both still be alive? Walking around this campus right now. Laughing. Flirting. Living. Cheyenne had said as much in the e-mail she'd sent me the night she died.

Ignore the note. You did this to me. You ruined my life.

Dead. Because of me.

"Crummy day," Constance Talbot said, hugging her tweed coat closer to herself as the wind whipped her red hair back from her face. The cold September sky above was gray, muddled, threatening rain as we crossed the quad at the center of the Easton Academy campus, together with our Billings housemates. Saturday it had been seventy-five degrees. Now, two days later, it was fifty-five. Had to love that temperamental New England weather. Constance cuddled her chubby, freckled cheeks into her collar and stared at the cobblestone path to the dining hall. At times like this I could easily imagine what she had looked like as a child. Precious. Vulnerable. Innocent.

"I'm glad my coat arrived on Saturday," Sabine DuLac said. Her new coat, befitting her unique style, was white and light blue brocade with old-fashioned cut-glass buttons. It contrasted beautifully with her dark hair and light brown skin. "It was cold in Boston," she added.

Right. Sabine had visited her sister in Boston over the weekend. I had completely forgotten to ask her how it had gone—how her sister was. Some friend I was. I'd have to remember to ask her later.

"It was freezing here, too. And we ended up spending a lot of time outside the dorm," Constance said.

"Because it was too depressing?" I asked.

We had, after all, only found Cheyenne's body on Saturday morning. Just two days ago. I could understand why everyone might be avoiding Billings House. Like Sabine, I had left campus and spent the weekend in New York with my boyfriend, Josh Hollis. I hadn't wanted to come back, but I'd had no choice. Billings was my home. These girls, most of whom were now gathered around me for warmth as we walked to breakfast, were like my family. For better or worse.

"Well, that, and the cops were all over the place," Tiffany Goulbourne said as she checked some setting on her tiny digital camera. "Going through Cheyenne's stuff, taking pictures of her room . . ."

"Why?" I asked. I had arrived home from the city late the night before and had yet to hear any of this.

"To confirm it was a suicide," Tiffany said, looking ill. Her long white coat blew open and billowed out behind her, but she didn't even seem to notice. She was one of those girls who was able to look perfect whether it was ten thousand degrees and humid or windy and pelting sleet. Tall and ebony-skinned with short-cropped black hair and big brown eyes, she had the cheekbones of a supermodel but preferred to spend her time behind the camera rather than in front of it, a quirk that almost none of the Billings Girls could understand. "Guess after last year they're being cautious. Want to make sure there's no question."

"They even asked us about you, Reed," Astrid Chou said in her cool British accent, her short black hair blowing straight up in the back. "About your row with Cheyenne."

"What?" I blurted, my heart pounding. "They don't think I—"

"No! No," Astrid said, first adamantly, then comfortingly. She put her hand on my arm and looked at me with her steady dark eyes. Astrid was a new transfer this year, but I had met her last December at Cheyenne's Christmas party in Litchfield. For a while I had thought she and Cheyenne were BFFs, but it had turned out that Astrid was more of a kindred spirit than I had thought. Like me, she hadn't condoned Cheyenne's crazy hazing tactics or her arbitrary ostracizing of some of the other new Billings Girls. I had a feeling she could turn out to be a great friend. Plus, her quirky style and honest, blunt sense of humor were both welcome anomalies in Billings.

"We told them it was just a normal fight between girls," Tiffany clarified. "Nothing weird. Happens all the time. Of course they don't think that you had anything to do with anything."

"They just had to ask," Sabine added. "It's their job."

Even in the face of all this logic, I had to stop. My heart was pounding in my very eyes. It was a suicide. A suicide. I had proof. I had her second suicide note on my computer—not that I was eager to share that with my friends or the police. And okay, according to that second note, which Cheyenne had e-mailed only to me, it had been my fault. But I hadn't actually *killed* her. This was insane.

As my closer friends paused around me, waiting for me to recover from my aneurysm, a few of the other Billings Girls rushed ahead to get out of the cold.

"Reed, no one thinks you had anything to do with this," Constance said. "Don't worry."

I swallowed hard. "But they actually thought she might have been . . ." I couldn't even say the word. Not again. Not again.

Tiffany swallowed and pressed her full lips together. "I guess they thought maybe."

I couldn't move. Murdered? They had thought Cheyenne might have been murdered? But why? What would make them think someone would want her dead? Besides me, of course. And our argument. But that hadn't been my fault. She had tried to steal my boyfriend.

The distinctly metallic rev of a power saw cut through the air. Everyone on the quad paused. A flock of birds took flight from a nearby oak, squawking like mad and scattering bright orange leaves all over the grass. Suddenly my heart was in my throat. I wondered how long it would be before I felt safe on campus again.

"What the hell was that?" Tiffany asked. She lifted her camera to capture a shot of the fleeing birds, never missing an opportunity to create art.

There was already a crowd of students gathered around the propped-open back door to Mitchell Hall, a central building just to the north of the dining hall, which housed the Great Room, several meeting rooms, and the art cemetery, among other things. We all hurried forward. There wasn't much that happened at Easton Academy that the Billings Girls didn't know about first. What was going on?

A few people slipped through the back door and down the wide hall, following the sounds of pounding and sawing and shouting, but I hesitated at the threshold. The windows to the art cemetery were right there. My very proximity to them made my blood curdle.

Josh and Cheyenne. Josh and Cheyenne. Josh and—

"Reed? Come on!"

Rose Sakowitz grabbed my hand and practically yanked my arm out of its socket. She was freakishly strong for someone so petite. But then, she did spend much of her free time in the state-of-the-art Easton gym or competing on the tennis team. I averted my eyes from the art cemetery door and focused on her bouncing red curls as we followed the crowd down the hall. To the left were the double doors that led to the Great Room. To the right was the large, octagonal solarium with its huge windows that overlooked the perfectly manicured Easton grounds. The room was peppered with leather couches and lined with packed mahogany bookshelves, potted plants, and Oriental carpets. It was supposed to be a place for students to gather and mingle, but there was no television or pool table or any other form of amusement, aside from the literary classics, and I had never known anyone to hang out there. Until now. Half the student body seemed to be gathered in the center of the room—where all the furniture was covered in plastic—gaping at the seven construction workers pounding away near the back wall.

"What's this all about?" Tiffany asked, moving forward to snap a few pictures.

"You guys haven't heard?" Missy Thurber asked, bringing up the rear.

"Heard what?" I asked.

Missy gave me her patented smirk and lifted her nose so high in the air I was pretty sure I could see her tonsils through those massive nostrils of hers. "Amberly Carmichael. She goes here now," she said, brushing her thick blond braid behind her shoulders.

"No way," Constance said.

"How did we not know this?" Tiffany asked.

"Who is Amberly Carmichael?" I asked.

They all laughed and Missy rolled her eyes. She pretty much

lived to roll her eyes at me. "Amberly Carmichael—of the Seattle Carmichaels?" she said. "Reed, come on. Even you must know who she is."

Missy clucked her tongue. I was starting to wonder what would happen if I shoved my fingers up her nose and pulled.

"Amberly's father is Dustin Carmichael. Founder and CEO of Coffee Carma? You've heard of *that*, right?" she said, adjusting the strap of her quilted Vera Bradley tote.

"You have to know Coffee Carma," Lorna Gross echoed. She was always echoing Missy. Last year I hadn't even been sure if Lorna had her own personality, she'd been so busy parroting Missy's every word, move, and wardrobe choice. Lately, however, she'd been displaying a tad more backbone. Maybe it was because of her new nose, or the fact that she'd tamed the frizz factor in her hair, or the fact that she was now a Billings Girl—I wasn't sure, but something had given her more confidence. For the moment, however, she'd fallen back into her bad Missy-mimicking habit.

"Of course I have," I replied. There was a Coffee Carma on every corner in America, even in my lame-ass hometown of Croton, Pennsylvania.

"Well, Dustin wrote a check to Easton at the beginning of the year. A check with a lot of zeroes. His only stipulation was that he wanted them to build a Coffee Carma on campus, so . . ." Missy lifted her palm, gesturing to the construction behind her.

"Good to know our new headmaster can be bought," Tiffany said under her breath.

"We're getting a Coffee Carma?" Vienna Clark shrieked, grasping London Simmons's arm. "Omigod! What have I been saying every morning for the past three years?"

"That you would *kill* for an iced caramel macchiato with extra whip?" London replied happily, tossing her teased brown hair. The two of them grasped hands and squealed, jumping up and down.

London Simmons and Vienna Clark were the serious party girls of Billings, and they did everything together—they traveled together, got their highlights done together, went for seaweed wraps and Brazilian waxes and eyebrow threading together. They were both petite girls with ample chests who preferred clothes of the low-cut, miniskirted variety. Of the two, Vienna was slightly more intelligent, London slightly more moody, but other than that they were practically twins. The Twin Cities were basically harmless and fun to be around, but watching them and the rest of my friends now, I felt sick to my stomach. They were wide-eyed, excited, buzzing with the news. Didn't any of them remember what had happened this weekend? Could a classmate's suicide really be erased by the promise of overpriced legal stimulants?

"I can't believe they're doing this right now," I said. "Couldn't they have at least waited a week? Shouldn't we all be, I don't know, mourning?" The Twin Cities had been Cheyenne's classmates for three years. I couldn't believe I had been forced to point this out.

London and Vienna stopped bouncing and instantly became contrite.

"You're right," London said. "Cheyenne *so* would have loved this. Coffee Carma was her favorite."

"Speaking of Her Billionairess," Missy said under her breath.

We all turned around to find an impish girl with loose blond curls walking toward us, flanked by two clone-ish friends. She was "too matchy-matchy," a phrase Kiran Hayes used to throw around while critiquing outfits last year. Kiran hated it when a girl's clothing choices seemed overly planned, and she would send anyone committing this sartorial offense back to her room to change. Amberly's matchiness took the form of a black, gray, and red plaid skirt topped by a gray T-shirt and black cardigan. Her red Marc Jacobs bag was the same shade as the red cabbie hat perched jauntily atop her head. Her scarlet heels clicked on the marble floor as she walked right up to me and smiled.

"Hi, Reed!" she said.

Like she knew me. Like we were old friends.

"Hi . . . Amberly?" I replied uncertainly.

"Isn't it so exciting? A Coffee Carma right here on Easton's campus!"

"Yeah. It's great." Why was she talking to me?

"Here. My father said I could give a few of these out, but only to special friends," Amberly said, leaning toward me and lowering her voice. She took out a small plastic card with tie-dyed swirls all over it.

"Um, thanks. What is it?" I asked, running my fingers along the slippery edges.

"It's a Carma Card!" she said, clearly incredulous that I didn't know. "Flash that baby and it means free coffee for life!"

The Billings Girls started muttering around me, wondering, no doubt, why I deserved to be granted the holy grail of gift cards and they, apparently, did not. I wondered the same thing myself, but forced myself to smile at this odd little person.

"Wow. Thanks."

I waited for her to go away, but she didn't move.

"So. Have you seen Noelle?" Amberly asked. "I heard she finally got off probation."

My heart stopped pounding. All my friends fell silent as the grave. Yes, I had seen Noelle, just two nights ago in the city. And the encounter had left me completely freaked. Left me wondering what her plans were. Left me wondering if she somehow knew that I had been e-mailing Dash McCafferty, whom—I had been relieved to hear—was no longer her boyfriend. However, she hadn't shared the details of the breakup, hadn't even told me if it had been recent or if it had, perhaps, happened last year when she'd been arrested for her role in Thomas Pearson's murder. The whole thing had been surreal—exciting and confusing at the same time. I had yet to tell any of the Billings Girls about it, and wasn't sure I wanted to, because knowing them, they would grill me about every last detail, from her designer shoes to her current weight, until I screamed. So why was this stranger asking me about her?

"Um . . . no," I lied. "Haven't seen her."

"Oh. Well, if you do, tell her Amberly said hi," she told me with a smile. "Our families are very old friends," she added, touching my arm with her fingertips. I was suddenly so hot that I thought the plastic card in my hand might melt and fuse to my skin. So that was why she'd given me the card above anyone else. She knew I was friends with the ever-powerful Noelle Lange.

"Oh. Okay," I replied shiftily. "Again, thanks for this."

"My pleasure," she replied, the smile widening. She had a row of perfectly white, square teeth. "I'll see you around."

She fluttered her fingers and strode away, hips wagging slightly beneath her plaid skirt. Her friends, who hadn't said a word or changed expression the entire time, scurried off behind her.

"What was that all about?" Missy sniffed the moment Amberly was gone.

"I have no idea," I replied.

"So have you really not heard from Noelle?" Rose asked me. "Not at all?"

"You know what, guys? I'm starving," I said quickly. "Let's just go to breakfast."

I turned toward the door and was met by a seriously red-cheeked Gage Coolidge, storming toward me like his pants were on fire. His usually gelled-up hair had been tossed around by the wind, and half of it was plastered to his forehead. He wore trendy jeans, trendier sneakers, and a thick gray sweater that highlighted his wide shoulders and lithe form. Boy would have been hot if his soul wasn't made of tar.

"Well, we're screwed," he said, his jaw clenched. Now that he was within sniffing distance, his semisour aftershave overwhelmed me. I had to take a step back to keep breathing.

"What's the matter?" Sabine asked, stepping forward. She'd had a crush on Gage since the beginning of the year—something I could neither comprehend nor thwart, no matter how hard I tried.

"I just got a text from my friend at Chapin," he said, whipping open his phone as proof. "Cheyenne's father canceled the Legacy!"

There was a general gasp from those around us, like a bomb had just gone off outside.

"What!?" Portia Ahronian snapped. She snatched the cell phone from him and gaped at it, raising her other, perfectly manicured hand to her chest, where it rested just below her omnipresent collection of gold necklaces. The gold offset her olive skin and dark hair to perfection, but in my opinion she could have cut back on the multitude of chains by one or two.

"Wait. How does Cheyenne's dad get to cancel the Legacy?" I asked. As far as I knew, the Legacy was a yearly party dating back decades. All the East Coast private schools were involved, and last year the party on Park Avenue had been attended by thousands. Only students who could claim to be third-generation private school attendees were invited, and your history had to go back much further than that in order to get a plus one. According to Walt Whittaker, with whom I'd attended the event last fall (since I was the first person in my family ever to set foot in a private school, I'd needed him to get me in), the same family had been hosting it for years.

"The Dreskins finally bailed," Rose explained. "Said they couldn't handle the insurance liability anymore. So Cheyenne begged her father to step in and host. It was her pet project, and Cheyenne's dad never said no to her, so . . ."

"Why didn't she tell us?" Tiffany asked.

"She wanted it to be a surprise. She only told me once the plans were set. She just couldn't keep it in anymore," Rose replied. "It was supposed to be at the Litchfield house."

Rose and Cheyenne had been roommates the year before, and Rose had been closer to Cheyenne than anyone else in the house. Their friendship had made it all the more difficult for her to side with me during the whole hazing fiasco, I knew.

"And now we're totally screwed," Gage said, wrenching his phone from Portia's grasp. "God. Cheyenne knew her dad was throwing this thing. Couldn't she have at least waited till effing November to off herself?"

The sudden angry peel of the electric saw felt as if it were piercing right through my brain. "What did you just say?"

Gage looked at me, his eyes wide with mock innocence. "What? I'm just saying."

"You're sick, you know that?" I snapped. "All of you are sick! Cheyenne's dead, for God's sake! And all you can think about are coffee bars and parties? What's the matter with you?"

No one answered me. Tiffany hid behind her camera, taking pictures of the work in progress. Constance's cheeks turned pink, Portia toyed with her necklaces, Sabine fiddled with the glass buttons on her coat, and Rose appeared close to tears. London and Vienna looked at each other, disturbed, as if I were the one embarrassing them. Well, fine. If I was so humiliating to have around, I would just leave them to their wallowing. I couldn't look at them right now anyway.

POOR LITTLE RICH GIRLS

Cheyenne's memorial service was scheduled for Saturday. Her father had called Rose and given her the info, which she had scribbled on a piece of yellow stationery and left on the table in the parlor. It was propped up against the vase of fresh flowers the cleaning staff replaced every week, and there it stayed, staring out at us like a message of doom. Now not only were we avoiding the end of the hall where Cheyenne's room was located, we were avoiding the parlor as well. Result? The Billings Girls were spending a lot more time in the library than we usually did this time of year.

Suddenly I couldn't wait for Coffee Carma to open. At least then we'd have somewhere else to congregate.

"Why must we study calculus?" Sabine whispered on Wednesday evening, dropping back in her seat. All fifteen of us were gathered around the long table that took up most of the aisle between philosophy and religion. The head of the table had been left open. Cheyenne's chair. I couldn't stop staring at it. "It shouldn't be a required subject. It means nothing unless you want to go to med school."

"I love calculus," I replied, happy for a distraction from the empty seat. I took a deep breath of that library air, letting the musty book smell fill my senses. Somehow, I always found that scent soothing.

Portia dropped her hand, her gold watch smacking against the wooden table. "You are *so* F.O.S," she said, lifting her thick hair over her shoulder. "No one likes calculus."

"F.O.S.?" I asked, looking at Rose. Portia hated it when anyone asked her to decipher her strange abbreviations. Maybe if she issued us all our own Ahronian-to-English dictionaries, we could keep up.

"Full of . . . you know," Rose whispered, her cheeks turning pink.

"Ah." Rose never cursed unless she absolutely had to.

"Anyway, Cheyenne liked calculus," Rose said. "She liked math in general. Something about it being unsubjective."

Lately, Cheyenne's name was the ultimate conversation killer. Everyone stopped talking—everyone except London and Vienna, who were sitting across from each other at the far end of the table. In the fresh silence their voices carried like shouts over open water.

"I know, I know! Your gown is perfection. It so sucks that you're not going to get to wear it," Vienna said.

"I mean, why did we even go to Milan this summer if the Legacy was gonna get canceled?" London whined, crossing her arms over her chest. "Two weeks couture-hopping in that ridiculous heat, and for what?"

"Well, you did get to meet Fabrizio," Vienna reminded her, lifting her perfect brows.

"Ah . . . Fabrizio," they both said wistfully, looking off into the stacks.

"What is the matter with you two?" I demanded, my eyes darting again to Cheyenne's empty seat.

Kiki Thorpe tugged her ever-present earbuds out of her ears and sat up straight, her heavy black boots slamming into the floor. Her blue eyes darted hungrily back and forth between the Twin Cities and me as she popped her gum, sensing impending conflict. "Catfight?" she asked with interest.

"No," I replied. "No catfight."

Kiki sighed in disappointment and sat back again. She tugged her pink bangs up until they stood straight out from her head, her eyes practically crossing as she looked up at them.

"It's just . . . this is really what you're talking about?" Sabine asked the Twin Cities, backing me up.

London and Vienna looked at us with a mild sense of distaste. Vienna rolled her eyes and turned to face us. "Don't make us out to be the villains here, okay?" she said, pressing her finger and its perfectly shaped nail into her open-but-ignored notebook. "You know you all wish the Legacy was happening even though Cheyenne's . . . gone. We're just the only ones who are woman enough to say it."

Everyone at the table looked at everyone else. Aside from Sabine and Constance, they all guiltily agreed with their eyes—even Rose, who had seemed more broken up about Cheyenne's death than anyone.

"Maybe if we talked to Mr. Martin about it. Maybe if he saw how much it meant to Cheyenne's friends, he'd change his mind," Vienna suggested.

"I don't think so," I replied.

I could just picture it: Cheyenne's dad sitting alone in his study, trying to pick out a coffin for his child. Suddenly the phone rings, and there's Vienna, pleading for him to throw a party for us, because Cheyenne would have wanted it that way. Man would probably drive out to Easton and strangle the girl himself. His daughter had taken her own life. Every time I thought about it, my heart swelled painfully, and tears prickled at the corners of my eyes. I couldn't imagine what he was feeling.

"Why not? It's worth a try," Portia replied. "I had the whole weekend planned with Hamilton, and now he's talking about saving his frecs."

"Frecs?" I asked.

"Frequent flyer miles," Tiffany explained. She placed her camera aside and pulled out her leather portfolio, filled with her latest prints.

Nice boyfriend. Is he more interested in you or the free-flowing drugs and sex-capades? Maybe it was time for a relationship evaluation. A re-eval, to put it in terms Portia might understand.

"I really think we should try calling Mr. Martin. Maybe he'd be happy to have something fun to focus on!" London suggested hopefully. "You know, something to take his mind off what happened."

"I don't think one little party is going to take his mind off the fact that his only daughter is dead," I said flatly. I mean, really, people.

"It's not a *little* party, Reed. We're talking about the Legacy here," Portia said. "It's, like, bigger than X-mas."

That was how she said it. *Ex-mas.* I had no response to that.

"Maybe someone else could throw it. Tiff? What about your dad? Tassos is always up for a party, isn't he?" London suggested.

Tiffany chuckled. "I so love that my father has a rep."

Tiffany's dad was the uni-named Tassos, an internationally renowned celebrity photographer who had been paid gazillions of dollars to photograph everyone from the Prince of Wales to Britney Spears's dogs. I had never met him, but he was one of the rare Easton dads who called his daughter at least once a week and chatted with her for hours at a time. Most girls in Billings, whose dads were too busy to recall they'd ever procreated, were jealous not only of Tassos's worldwide fame and Tiffany's many celebrity connections, but of their father-daughter relationship. Of course, I talked to my dad once a week as well, but being that I was from a middle-class family in central Pennsylvania, no one ever seemed surprised by that. Like my family was automatically assumed to be functional. If only they knew. I mean, maybe it was more functional lately, since my mom had cleaned herself up and stopped with the painkillers, but this time last year? The Brennan clan had been on a serious downward spiral.

"Well?" Portia asked.

"Sorry, girls, but the town house isn't big enough, the Sag Harbor house is under renovation, and I don't see everyone flying to Miami or Crete," Tiffany replied as she flipped through her portfolio.

"I'll fly to Crete!" Vienna announced. A few of the others murmured their assent.

"Listen, you guys, the Legacy isn't happening this year, okay? Just get used to it," I said. I picked up my pencil and returned to my assignment, hoping that would put an end to it.

"You're just bitter because you wouldn't be able to go anyway," Missy said, her eyes flicking over me in that derisive way of hers.

She was, of course, correct about that. I had only been able to attend last year as Walt Whittaker's date—well before he was Constance's boyfriend, of course. Josh didn't qualify for plus-one status, so even if the Legacy did happen, I'd be spending the biggest night of the year watching reruns of *The Closer* on the plasma in the parlor.

"Wait, so you mean you can go?" I asked Missy. "You didn't go last year."

"I had something better to do," Missy said, averting her eyes.

"Oh, please. Your mom forbid you from going till you were sixteen," Lorna blurted. We all laughed, and Lorna earned herself a look of death that sent her hiding behind her chemistry text.

"This is just unacceptable," Portia said. "Cheyenne was all about tradition, and the Legacy was one of her favorite nights of the year. If the Legacy was canceled because of her, she would hate it. I mean, not having the Legacy is like dishonoring her memory."

Honestly? She kind of had a point there. Cheyenne would have hated to know that a tradition as hallowed as the Legacy was compromised because of something she had done.

There was a loud laugh from the next aisle over, and suddenly Ivy Slade appeared at the head of the table. With her raven hair pulled back from her angular face, her big silver, straight-drop earrings, and her flowy black baby-doll dress, she looked way too sophisticated for the library. Even the Billings Girls knew to dress down slightly for a study session.

"You people are unbelievable," she said. "Poor little rich girls can't have their party? Aw. How pathetic. One of your best friends just killed herself, and this is all you can talk about?"

"Shut up, Ivy," Portia snapped. "You didn't even like Cheyenne."

Ivy glared at Portia with such venom that I half expected Portia's gold necklaces to turn green and rot. Then Ivy sort of straightened up, a smirk lighting her otherwise pale face.

"You're right. I didn't," she said, placing her hands on the back of Cheyenne's empty chair. "So what does it tell you that I seem to care more about the fact that she's dead than you do?

Her gaze slid over table in silent judgment before she turned and strode away. Suddenly I found myself staring at that empty chair again, my heart heavier than a concrete slab. I had pretty much detested Ivy Slade from the first time I spoke to her, but right then I couldn't have agreed with her more.

THE PARTY MUST GO ON

Since the beginning of the year, the Ketlar Hall advisor, Mr. Cross, had been leaving campus for three hours every Friday night for some unknown reason (AA meetings? A torrid affair? Karaoke night at the Boar's Nest?), leaving the dorm that housed the most coveted guys on campus unguarded. The pattern had just recently been confirmed by the boys of Ketlar as unwavering and therefore useful. So that Friday night, it was as if a Marc Jacobs sample sale were being held in the upperclassman boys' dorm. Females from all corners of campus descended on the place, giggling and chatting in excitement, their four-hundred-dollar heels click-clacking on the lobby floor.

I was one of them, of course, but I wasn't giggling or chatting, and my sneakers merely squeaked. I found Josh kicked back on his unmade bed in his room, which was wallpapered on his side with his own paintings, and on Trey Prescott's side with posters of famous European footballers. Josh's blond curls looked as unruly and touchable as ever, and he wore rumpled jeans and a white long-sleeved tee, which highlighted not only his perfect pecs, but what was left of his summer tan. Trey had kindly vacated the premises, having no girlfriend to fool around with at present, so Josh and I tried to get down to the reason we were there, but I was too distracted to concentrate. As was Josh, apparently. After attempting to make out on his bed for fifteen minutes, we both sat back and sighed. My back rested against the wall next to his bed. He leaned into his headboard. We shot each other apologetic smiles and looked away.

This was totally insane. Here I was with the most beautiful guy on campus—a guy who loved me so much I could see it in his gorgeous blue eyes every single time he looked at me—and yet the only thing I could think about was that e-mail from Cheyenne.

And about the Legacy.

And Noelle.

And Dash.

What the hell had Noelle meant when she'd said, "Everything happens for a reason?" Was it just a coincidence that Dash had typed the very same words to me in his last e-mail? Was it something that they both liked to say? Or did Noelle somehow know about my secret correspondence with her ex-boyfriend?

Suddenly I started to sweat. I shoved my hands into my long brown hair and pushed it back from my face. I couldn't think about this. Not now. Not with Josh's legs resting over mine and his paint-speckled fingers toying with the strap on the hip of my cargo pants.

"Hey. Are you okay?" he asked me.

"Fine. Why?" I replied.

"You looked like you were having deep thoughts," Josh said, reaching up to tuck a stray lock of hair behind my ear. "What are you thinking about?"

Oh, I'm thinking about my secret e-mail relationship with Dash McCafferty. And about how it's not only a betrayal of you, but of Noelle—because even if they're not together, she must still consider him hers. And about how if she finds out about it, she's going to kick my ass into next semester.

No. Not if. When. When she finds out about it. Because who am I kidding, here? This is Noelle Lange we're talking about. I wouldn't be surprised it the girl had top secret clearance at the freaking Pentagon. She always knows everything.

Also, I'm thinking about Cheyenne, and the fact that you cheated on me with her. And the fact that I called her a whore and a hundred other nasty things. And the fact that she subsequently killed herself and blamed it on me. My heart constricted and my eyes welled. I looked away, willing myself to chill.

"Reed?" Josh prompted.

"Sorry. I was thinking about the Legacy," I told him, figuring it was the safest topic. I took a deep breath and stared straight ahead, not ready to give him a good look at my probably blotchy face quite yet.

There was a long pause. Too long. Then Josh drew his legs back, curling them up story style, and pushed both hands back through his dark blond curls—all of which snapped right back into place. Suddenly, no part of him was touching any part of me. Misjudgment, thy name is Reed.

"The Legacy?" he asked. His very tone was a reprimand. His mouth twisted into a frown of distaste. Like it soured his tongue to even say the words.

"Yeah. It's pretty much all my friends can talk about right now," I told him. "Not me, but them. Everyone's pretty crushed that it got canceled."

Josh scoffed. "Why am I not surprised?"

Instantly I felt defensive. Even though I agreed with him. That was just the way I was when it came to the Billings Girls. Just call me the devil's advocate.

"I know," I said, turning to face him. "But for some of them this is the most important event of the year."

Bigger than X-mas.

"That in and of itself is sad," Josh said. He shoved himself up and crossed over to the easel at the foot of his bed, where he rather vehemently began to sort through pots of paint and crusty paint-brushes. "How can they be thinking about getting wasted and party-ing, when Cheyenne just died?"

"Well . . . some people use that stuff as escape mechanisms, don't they?" I asked facetiously.

"Yeah. That's a great way to cope," Josh replied, just as facetiously.

"I'm not saying *I'm* gonna do that—I'm just trying to understand where they're coming from," I replied, my voice rising a bit as I scooted to the edge of his bed. "The same thing happened last year when Thomas died, remember? All anyone wanted was to figure out a way to get their minds off what had happened."

"Right. Because God forbid anyone at this school ever has to actually deal with something," Josh snapped. "Why are you always blindly defending those people?"

"Why is it so hard for you accept the fact that *those people* are my friends?" I shot back.

I loved Josh, but one thing about him that always irked me was his venomous disapproval of the Billings Girls. Even though in this case I understood where he was coming from, he didn't have to act as though they were so predictable and so awful all the time. And I hated the fact that he tended to lump them all in together—as if good people like Constance, Sabine, Tiffany, and Rose were somehow just as evil as Ariana Osgood had turned out to be the year before. Maybe sometimes their priorities weren't always the same as ours, but that didn't make them bad people. There was still a lot of good in them—good he refused to see. And they were my friends. Most of them, anyway. I was sick of him attacking them at every turn.

Josh sighed and looked down at his bare feet, gripping a few brushes in both hands. "I'm sorry. It's not you, it's just . . . Imagine what Cheyenne would think. How she would feel if she knew that this was what her friends were talking about four days after she died?"

Just hearing him express compassion for Cheyenne's feelings stung. I know it's petty, but less than two weeks ago I'd found the two of them getting hot and heavy in the art cemetery on the very day we'd both said "I love you" for the first time. It had turned out that Cheyenne had drugged Josh to get him in the mood, so to speak, and I'd forgiven him. And yes, the girl was dead now. But none of that made the memory of her straddling him half naked, of the way he was looking at her like she was some kind of bodacious sex goddess, hurt any less.

"Honestly? I think she'd be proud," I said, lifting my chin slightly. Even though I hadn't voiced my agreement at the time, Portia's argument at the library had been the only one that made sense to me. Cheyenne would have hated to be remembered as the girl who had torpedoed the Legacy. If anyone else in our circle had died, Cheyenne would have certainly taken a "the party must go on" stance.

Josh's face screwed up in consternation. "Proud?"

"Yeah. Cheyenne was all about Easton and tradition. She *loved* being one of the longest legacies on campus," I told him. "I think she'd want the Legacy to go on, and I think she'd be upset that her dad canceled it. You knew Cheyenne pretty well, and I'm just trying to think like her," I said, trying to hide my disgust, once again, at the thought of the two of them. "Don't you think that's true?"

"Wow," Josh said, staring at me.

"What?" I replied, feeling uncertain.

"They've totally brainwashed you over there," he replied.

My mouth dropped open. Considering how he felt about them, lumping me in with the Billings Girls in his mind was pretty much the worst insult he could lob at me.

"I'm going to go now," I said, grabbing my keys.

"Reed. Wait. I'm sorry. I didn't mean—"

"Yes, you did," I replied.

Then I yanked open the door and put an end to our not-so-romantic night.

GLITCH

I stared at the ceiling in my room at Billings that night, listening to Sabine's light breathing, unable to even fathom sleep. During the day I could sometimes ignore it, sometimes shove it aside—distract myself with other things. But when the lights were out and I was alone, the thoughts came, and I couldn't stop them.

How does a person decide to die? Isn't it the thing we're all most afraid of? I mean, when you think about it . . . when you really think about it . . . it's the one thing about life that you simply cannot imagine. Because no one knows what it's really like. No one knows where you go. You can't just take it back once it's done and be hanging out with your friends a couple of days later and say, "So, was it totally weird when I died?" That's just it. Even if there is an afterlife, life as you know it is just over.

Cheyenne was just over.

I sat straight up in bed, my heart pounding. It was the night before

Cheyenne's memorial service, and I hadn't slept in two days. Every time I even started to close my eyes, I would see her pretty, pert face and would suddenly jolt awake. I couldn't take much more of this. It had taken months for the nightmares and unbidden daydreams about Thomas to peter out. How long would it take before Cheyenne's suicide stopped haunting me? Would it ever?

The lines of her e-mail were burned indelibly into my brain. She had blamed me for her death. Blamed *me*. How could that ever be okay?

I shoved the covers aside and cool air rushed over my hot legs. My hair was plastered to the back of my head with sweat. I had to do something to distract myself. E-mail my brother. Or Natasha Crenshaw, my roommate from last year. Something. Glancing at Sabine's bed, I got up and opened my laptop, then pulled the chair back from the desk as quietly as I could. Out of habit, I opened my inbox first. There was a message from Dash right at the top. My heart pounding for a whole new reason, I clicked it open.

> Dear Reed,
>
> I heard about Cheyenne's memorial service. I really wish I could go, but I can't make it. I feel awful, considering how long I've known Cheyenne, but I have this massive paper due on Monday, and unfortunately, funeral services for casual friends don't merit an extension here at Yale. But don't worry. I'm sure you'll be fine. It'll suck, don't get me wrong, but you'll get through it. I know your Billings friends

will be there for you, and I'm sure you'll keep yourself busy being there for them as well. You've always been good at that—being there for your friends no matter what.

If it does get tough, just know that I'll be thinking about you all day . . . wishing I was there with you.

Love,

Dash

There was no air in the room. I read the e-mail over three times and my heart felt full. That line about me and my Billings friends—how he knew we'd be there for one another—I couldn't stop staring at it.

Dash understood. He knew what my friends meant to me. He knew what Billings meant. Not like Josh. Josh, who felt the need to bash my housemates at every available opportunity. Dash understood, and it made me feel validated. Proud. Happy.

And then there was that final line.

I'll be thinking about you . . . wishing I was there with you. There was no misreading that. And he'd signed the e-mail "Love." *Love, Dash.* In one e-mail, everything between us had changed. It had just gotten interesting.

And dangerous. And wrong.

Josh was my boyfriend. And Noelle was one of my best friends.

So why couldn't I stop smiling?

Fingers trembling, I rested my fingers lightly on the keys. Everything hinged on what I typed back. I could tell him I'd be thinking of

him, too. Could take this thing, whatever it was, to the next level. Or
I could ignore what he'd said. I could be cold and distant and loyal to
Josh. Dash would get the hint. He wasn't a dumb guy.

That was what I should do. Obviously that was what I should do.
Things had been strained between me and Josh tonight, sure, but it
didn't matter. It was going to get better eventually. I loved him. He
loved me. I couldn't jeopardize that for an e-mail flirtation with a guy
who lived hundreds of miles away. Even if he had just made me feel
infinitely better with one e-mail, while earlier tonight Josh had made
me feel like crap.

My face flushed hot, remembering Josh's obstinacy. I didn't want
to go there. Didn't want to dwell on the negative. I wanted to dwell on
this new, calm, validated feeling. I typed back. . . .

Dash,
   I'll be wishing you were there with me too.

Sabine shifted in her bed, letting out a sigh. My hands jumped
from the keyboard as if the keys had just turned white hot. I glanced
over my shoulder tremulously, but Sabine had simply rolled over. She
wasn't glaring at me in admonishment. Even if she knew whom I was
e-mailing, she wouldn't know that it was wrong. And was it wrong,
really? Dash was my friend. Plus, I needed a distraction from everything. The weirdness with Josh, the confusion over Cheyenne—I
needed something light to get me through all the dark.

I took a deep breath, signed the e-mail "Love, Reed," and sent it

on its way. And I didn't even feel guilty. All I felt was tired. Excruci-
atingly, permanent-yawn-in-the-back-of-my-throat tired. I closed
the "mail sent" window, and my inbox automatically popped up.
There was a new e-mail at the top of the list. I did a double take. My
heart was sucked right out of my body, and I gripped the desk as I
buckled forward.

The e-mail was from Cheyenne.

No. No, no, no, no, no. This was not possible. What the hell was
going on here? *Delete it. Just delete it. It's not really there anyway. You're
just hallucinating. Imagining things. You're exhausted. Delusional. Delete
it and go to sleep.*

But how could I? It was a week to the day the first e-mail had been
sent. A week since she'd died. I had to open it. I had to know.

Holding my breath, feeling like I was about to shake apart at the
seams, I clicked open the message.

Ignore the note. You did this to me. You ruined my life.

Every cell in my body went cold. I couldn't breathe. I gripped the
edge of my desk to keep myself from fainting or reeling—just to feel
something solid and real. Because this . . . this e-mail . . . it couldn't
be real. It couldn't be happening. It was the same message I'd received
last weekend. Cheyenne's last e-mail. How had it been re-sent? Had
someone sneaked into her room? Was someone on her computer,
messing with me?

With a sudden surge of adrenaline, I shoved myself away from my desk and tiptoed to the door. Every inch of me quaked as I slipped out into the hallway. Cheyenne's room was just a few doors down. I looked for the glow of a light under the door, but there was none. Still, that didn't mean there wasn't someone inside. Sitting at her computer. Having a bit of fun at my expense. I took a deep breath, held it, and started to walk.

The hallway had never felt so wide, so frigid, so silent. As I passed by the grainy photos of Easton Academy through the years, I felt as if someone was watching me. As if at any moment cold hands would reach out and grab me. Clearly, I had seen too many horror movies. I had to get a grip. When I made it to Cheyenne's room, I pressed my palms into the wood trim around the door and breathed.

Someone's in there. Someone has to be in there. I'm not crazy. That e-mail did not send itself. Squelching the fear that threatened to overcome me, I held my breath and opened the door.

It swung wide and fast, as if propelled by a burst of wind. The room was empty, the computer dark.

No one was there.

For a long moment I stood alone, disbelieving. If no one had sent it, how had it shown up in my inbox? How could it possibly have happened? No answer miraculously came to me, and the longer I stood there, the more the room in front of me came into focus. I started to notice things. Things I hadn't noticed the last time I had been there—that morning when we found Cheyenne.

Like the suitcases, three of them, open on the floor near the far wall. There were sweaters piled into one, stacks of neatly folded lingerie in another. Cheyenne had started to pack that night. Had been getting ready to go.

At what point had she stopped? At what point had she decided that she was not, in fact, ever going to leave Billings? At least not alive.

I would never know.

Curiosity getting the better of me, I stepped into the room and closed the door quietly behind me. On her dresser was her makeup case, filled to the brim with Shiseido and Laura Mercier. Next to it sat a small silver box with ornate etching on the lid. Beautiful. Taking a closer look, I saw that there was a monogram worked into the swirling design. *VMS*, the letters all the same size. Why would Cheyenne Martin have a box with the initials *VMS* etched into it? Tentatively, I opened the box and froze. Inside, sitting on the black lining, was Cheyenne's diamond *B* necklace. I couldn't believe she had ever taken it off. This necklace symbolized everything important to her. Then I saw that something was wrong with the chain. It hadn't been unclasped. It had, in fact, been snapped. How? Why? Had she torn it off in the midst of a fit over being expelled?

Another thing I would never know.

Spooked by the violent image, I clicked the box closed and placed it right back where it had been. Right next to the pieces of the cell phone I had shattered against the wall above her bed in the midst of our Josh confrontation. She had gotten a new one the very next day, so why had she kept the remnants of the old one?

One more unanswered question.

Then I looked at her computer. She had sent that e-mail from this machine. Had used that keyboard to type her final message. Was it still in her system? If she'd sent it from here, it still had to be coming from here, didn't it? It had to be.

And then it hit me. Maybe she had set it up to be a repeating e-mail. Maybe she had set her server to send me her suicide note every Friday for the rest of my life. The very thought made the room tilt before me, and I grasped the desk.

Was she that sadistic? That angry? That unhinged? It couldn't be. But if it was set up that way . . . if it was, I had to stop it. If it was, I had to make it go away.

Before I could rethink my actions, I sat down in Cheyenne's pink upholstered desk chair and powered up her computer. It seemed to take forever to whir to life, and when it did I was faced with her desktop wallpaper, a photo of all of us taken last year in front of Billings on the last day of school. The sight of all those smiling, unsuspecting faces—Cheyenne's dead center—made my eyes sting. I quickly double clicked the Easton crest at the top right of the page, and the Easton e-mail system popped open.

That was when I froze. It was, of course, asking for her password.

Dammit. Damn all the damn security. How was I ever going to figure out Cheyenne Martin's password? Feeling as if I couldn't give up now, I typed a few obvious things. "Billings." Nope. "Easton." Nope. "Josh" and "Hollis." Nope. Thank God. But I was at a loss. Last year, when Dash and I had broken into Ms. Lewis-Hanneman's computer, he had used some universal password that Lance Reagan had cracked, but I had no idea what it was. I could have called Dash or Lance or Josh or any of the guys in Ketlar, all of whom, apparently, had been granted this information, but whoever I asked would want to know why I wanted it. It was no good. I was going to have to abort this mission. It was all I could do to keep from picking the monitor up and slamming it to the floor in frustration. But that, surely, would be loud enough to attract some attention.

Taking a deep, shaky breath, I turned off her computer. As soon as the room went dark, a floorboard creaked behind me. I whipped around, heart in my throat, but again, there was no one there. Nothing but Cheyenne's open closet.

I really was losing my mind, and this room wasn't helping. I quickly got up and slipped back to my room, sliding silently under the covers, which I drew all the way up to my chin. There would be no sleeping tonight, that much was now clear. I was just going to have to lie here and wait until morning. Until Cheyenne's memorial. Until it was time to say good-bye and maybe, just maybe, I could say good-bye to all this guilt and fear and uncertainty as well.

A girl could hope.

EULOGY

"My daughter always wore her heart on her sleeve. If you knew her, you knew her feelings, you knew her hopes, you knew her dreams," Mrs. Kane, Cheyenne's mother, said. She stood behind a small podium in front of a huge bank of windows that fronted the rocky Cape May shoreline. Before her, a hundred guests sat still as statues, not daring to move and disrupt the service. "But as her mother, I like to think that I knew her better than anyone, so today I'd like to share with you some little-known facts about Cheyenne Martin, my little girl."

I reached out and gripped Josh's hand. Every time Cheyenne's name was mentioned, all the hairs on my neck and arms stood on end. Ever since I had received her e-mail again the night before, I had felt shaky, vulnerable, almost as if I was being watched. That feeling had only intensified upon entering her mother's huge, airy Victorian on Cape May. Cheyenne's picture was everywhere. Staring at me. Judging me. Blaming me. As miserable as I had expected this

experience to be, it was ten times worse now. My own personal torture chamber.

"My little girl," Mrs. Kane repeated wistfully.

She placed her hands on the sides of the podium and paused as
we all held our breath. Cheyenne's mom was a slim blond woman
who could have doubled for Naomi Watts, but even with her wispy
body, she had a strength about her. She wore a formfitting black suit
and black heels, her hair back in a low bun, her makeup perfectly
applied. Behind her and to the left, hunched in a wooden chair, was
Cheyenne's father, who was not nearly as composed as his former
wife. He had a chiseled jaw, broad shoulders, and day-old stubble—
handsome even through his obvious grief.

"Cheyenne loved horses, as I'm sure you all know, but did you
know that her greatest dream as a child was to own a pink pony with a
red tail?" Mrs. Kane said.

The crowd laughed quietly and shifted in their seats.

"Many of you know that my daughter was also a philanthropist,
spending a few weeks each summer building houses with Habitat for
Humanity," Mrs. Kane continued. "But did you know that she learned
to love architecture and construction so much that she designed and
built a house for our dog Coco all on her own?"

Mr. Martin hung his head. Guilt surged through me, white hot
and fresh. I squeezed Josh's fingers again. Thank God he was there.
Steadfast, solid Josh. Josh, who hadn't mentioned a word of our
argument all morning. Who'd simply put his arm around me on the
quad, brought me to his car, and hadn't stopped asking if I was okay

all day long. Even in the midst of a fight, he cared about me enough to selflessly be there for me.

Why had I sent that e-mail to Dash last night? Why? I had done it in a moment of weakness. A moment of needing to be understood and comforted. But who was here for me now? Josh. All day long. Comforting. He was the guy I loved. The only guy I needed.

"And I'm sure you all know how much she loved her friends, the girls of Billings House." Here Mrs. Kane paused to smile down at us, Cheyenne's housemates. We were all seated in the first two rows, at her insistence, and I suddenly felt a glaring red spotlight burn my skin. "She loved you girls more than anything, and I know that if she were here with us today, she would tell you all how much she misses you, and that she hopes you all remember her for the things she did to brighten your life at Billings, and not for the way in which she left it."

Her eyes shone as she looked at each of us. A tear slid down my cheek and I shakily swiped it away. Cheyenne didn't miss me. She hated me. She wouldn't be dead if it weren't for me.

"Now, if you'll all adjourn to the shoreline outside . . . in a few minutes we'll be releasing Cheyenne's ashes at her favorite spot on the bluff. Thank you," Mrs. Kane said, mustering a bright smile.

The guests started to stir, but Mrs. Kane stepped around the podium and stopped Rose with a hand to her arm.

"Girls, would you mind staying back for a moment? There's something I'd like to say to you all," she said, looking me directly in the eye.

My heart plummeted. Why had she looked at me? Why me?

"You gonna be okay?" Josh asked, squeezing my hand.

There was an enormous lump in my throat, impossible to speak through, but I managed to nod.

"I'll wait right outside," he assured me, his blue eyes resolute.

"'Kay," I croaked.

I sat down again next to Kiki, who had hidden her pink bangs under a black cabbie pulled low over her brow. My heart pounded so hard, I was sure I was going to pass out. What could Cheyenne's mother possibly want to talk to us about?

"This should be interesting," Kiki said under her breath, popping her gum as she slumped down. Her heavy black boots peeked out from under the hem of her long gray skirt.

"This will only take a moment," Mrs. Kane began. She smiled as she clasped her hands in front of her. A rock the size of my head flashed on her ring finger. Mr. Martin, shoulders hunched, hovered behind her. "First, a request. Tomorrow morning, Cheyenne's father and I will be coming to Easton to pack up Cheyenne's things, but we've talked about it and we'd like for each of you to stop by her room tonight and choose something of our daughter's to keep."

Everyone looked at everyone else. She couldn't be serious.

Mr. Martin cleared his throat loudly. "We know how much you all meant to our . . . to Chey—" He paused and collected himself, running his hand over his eyes. "We know how much you all meant to her, and we know she'd want you all to have something to remember her by. So we hope you'll do us . . . do her memory . . . this honor. . . ."

He trailed off, looking at the floor, and shook his head. "I'm sorry. If you'll excuse me . . . ," he said, his voice cracking.

He rushed out of the room, hand to his mouth, his expensive pants swishing as he went. I had never felt so uncomfortable in my life. No one moved. To see a man like him break down in that way—it was awful. Horrifying. It brought the whole thing home all over again.

"Mrs. Kane. I'm so sorry," Rose said, standing tremulously. "I wish I . . . I wish—"

"Oh, Rose. Come here, honey," Cheyenne's mother said.

Rose stepped over everyone's legs, already crying, and Cheyenne's mother pulled her into a hug. No one knew what to do. We all just sat there, listening to the sound of Rose's muffled sobs.

Cheyenne's mother fished a tissue from her Chanel purse. She handed it to Rose, who pressed it to her nose shakily. "Girls, I know you're grieving, and you should be. You just lost one of your best friends. But I don't want any of you to waste time feeling guilty or asking 'what if.' None of you are responsible for my daughter's actions."

Except me.

"She loved you all so much. She loved that house so much," Mrs. Kane said. "She would want you to get on with your lives. She would want you to continue to uphold the Billings name and its traditions. Mourn her, honor her, but don't forget to live your lives too. Don't look back with regret."

I couldn't believe what I was hearing. Was Cheyenne's own mother trivializing her death? How could she expect us to move on? To have no regrets? The last year had been nightmare after nightmare for all of us. I glanced around, expecting everyone to look as appalled as I felt, but my blood ran cold. Instead, my friends seemed to be buying it. Already a few of them had visibly perked up. But then, I suppose I couldn't blame them. If Cheyenne's flesh and blood was excusing them from mourning, was telling them to get over their grief, who were they not to listen?

"Now, let's all go outside and join the others," Mrs. Kane said, giving Rose a squeeze. "I'm sure they're ready for us now."

After the briefest hesitation, everyone around me started to rise and file out of the room. My knees quaked as I got up, and I had to steady myself with a hand on the back of a chair.

"Reed? Are you okay?" Constance asked me.

"Yeah, I'm—"

"Reed Brennan?" Mrs. Kane interrupted, having overheard Constance. "I wasn't entirely sure it was you. You look so different in the pictures. . . ."

My heart all but stopped. Pictures? What pictures?

"I'm sorry?" I said.

A few of the Billings Girls shot us quizzical looks as they left the room, but only Sabine and Constance hung back, standing a respectful distance from myself and Cheyenne's mother.

"Cheyenne spoke so highly of you," Mrs. Kane said.

I blinked. "She did?"

"You're surprised," she stated, smoothing her already perfectly smooth hair back toward her bun. "But she did. When we were in Greece over the summer, she told me all about you. How you brought a much-needed dose of reality to Billings. How grounded you were. I think you were a good influence on her."

I couldn't have been more flabbergasted if she'd whipped out a flaming baton and started tap-dancing.

"I have something for you," Mrs. Kane said.

She turned and placed her bag on the podium so that she could search through it. I was so confused I felt weak. Was this really what Cheyenne had thought of me last year? It was hard to recall after all the bickering and venom of the past few weeks, but we *had* been friends. Had spent a lot of time together last spring.

But still, if she had ever thought I was grounded, and that I was "much needed" in Billings, then why had she spent so much time this year making sure I knew I didn't belong? Just over a week ago, she had told me flat out that I wasn't Billings material. That I would never understand what it meant to be there. What had happened since the summer that had changed her mind about me so drastically? Or had she not changed her mind at all? Maybe she'd just been so in love with Josh that she would have done or said anything to hurt me. Tried to get me to leave Billings so she wouldn't have to look at me anymore. She had to have had real feelings for him, right? You don't drug a guy into fooling around with you if your feelings are immoderate. Not that I would know from experience, but still.

"Here. I found this among her things," Mrs. Kane said turning around. She handed me a photo. It was a picture of Cheyenne and me taken at Vienna's Sweet Seventeen party last spring. The two of us were smiling broadly, hugging each other, our cheeks pressed together almost as if we were best friends. Because we had been friends. As difficult as it was to recall, we had been. It was a gorgeous shot, and

I remembered when Tiffany had taken it. We had been dancing to "Margaritaville" on the deck of the yacht, singing at the top of our lungs. I remembered being surprised that people in the Easton circle knew the words to a song like "Margaritaville," but I suppose tunes like that were universal. There was a pinhole in the top of the photo, as if Cheyenne had hung it somewhere. It had meant enough to her to put it on display. "She would have wanted you to have it."

A bubble rose in my throat, choking off my air supply.

"Remember what I said, Reed. Don't waste too much time ruminating on what's already done. You're young. You should live your life." She gave my shoulder a squeeze and started past me. Suddenly, the guilt crashed over me anew, and it was too much for me to bear.

"Mrs. Kane," I blurted.

She paused and turned to look at me expectantly. "Yes?"

"I . . . I'm so sorry," I said, my vision blurring as I looked at the picture. "I didn't mean—"

Constance stepped forward as if to hug me or steady me, and suddenly I snapped back to reality. What was I going to say? That I hadn't meant to force Cheyenne to kill herself? That I was sorry I had contributed to the death of her daughter? I looked at Constance and Sabine, both of whom were wide-eyed, concerned. What was I thinking? No one could know about that e-mail. No one.

"You didn't mean what, dear?" Mrs. Kane asked.

I swallowed hard and shoved the photo into my purse. "Nothing. I'm sorry. I'm just . . . really sorry."

Mrs. Kane smiled sympathetically. "Thank you, Reed."

She turned and strode out.

"I can't believe Cheyenne said all that stuff about you," Constance said, biting her lip.

"Yeah. Me neither," I replied, overwhelmed by my confusion, my guilt.

"We should probably go outside. They'll want to start soon," Sabine suggested, putting her arm around me.

So I walked out into the sunshine with my two closest friends, feeling completely detached from them. They didn't know what was really going on inside of me. Didn't know what I was capable of, what I had done. And they never would.

Even with them flanking me, comforting me, I had never felt so alone.

CLOSURE

Outside on the bluff, the pastor finished his speech, and Cheyenne's parents stepped forward to lift the gold urn from the white lace cloth on which it had been sitting during the service. They walked out onto the bluff with the container between them, walked out almost to the breakers, to where the water collided with the earth. Mrs. Kane said something to her ex-husband. He replied with a nod. Then he opened the urn and a huge cloud of black ash poured out, whipped up by the wind.

Behind me someone wailed. Rose dissolved into tears. I felt something inside of me start to shake. Like my ribs were crumbling around my heart. I clutched Josh's hand, and he immediately put his arm around me and held me tightly to his side. Whatever was trying to batter its way out of me, I held my breath and held it in.

On the bluff Mr. Martin dropped to his knees. The urn fell away and rolled until it hit Mrs. Kane's feet. Several people—family members, it seemed—moved forward to help. The rest of us watched the last of Cheyenne's ashes as they were scattered by the wind.

And then it was over. The last speck was gone, and the crowd began to disperse. I took a deep breath as Mr. Martin was helped to his feet, and tried to let the air fill me.

It was over. Done. We'd said good-bye. Much to my surprise, I felt a huge sense of relief. Maybe this was all I needed. Closure, or whatever they call it. Maybe I really would be able to move on.

"I can't believe Taylor and Kiran didn't show," Portia sniffed to her roommate, Shelby Wordsworth, as they walked by us. "They were initiated with us. I mean, how rude."

"Please. No one's heard from Miss Genius since last fall, and Kiran puts the 'self' in 'selfish,'" Shelby sniffed. "I am not at all surprised."

My face grew hot at her scathing words. Shelby was a senior, gorgeous in an understated, sophisticated way with her thick, dark blond hair, bright blue eyes, and refined clothing choices. But she had barely ever spoken two words to me. She hadn't been that close with my friends last year—with Noelle, Ariana, Kiran, and Taylor—so I felt as if she had no right to criticize them now. Even though technically she had known them longer than I had.

Still, it wasn't the time to criticize her. Instead, I glanced around, wondering if any of the former Billings Girls *had* shown up but were just keeping a low profile. I had thought of them that morning—considered that they might attend the service—but I had been so distracted during the eulogy and by Mrs. Kane's "no regrets" directive that I had forgotten all about them.

"So . . . you okay?" Josh asked me as we followed the rest of the Easton students down the hill. His dark blond curls had been tamed with gel, and in his pressed blue suit and dark tie, he'd never looked more perfect.

"Yeah, actually. I think I'll be all right." I bit my lip, hesitating. "So, are we going to talk about it? You know, the fight?"

Josh tipped his head back, his hands in his pockets. When he looked at me again, his expression was pragmatic. "I'm thinking no."

Relieved, I smiled. The last thing I needed was more drama. "No?"

"I say we chalk it up to emotions—temporary insanity—and move on," he suggested. "You think?"

"I am totally down with that plan," I replied. Temporary insanity. Perhaps that could double as my excuse for that e-mail to Dash. Yes. Temporary insanity worked. I liked that. I took a deep breath of the crisp sea air, feeling infinitely better as I started walking again. "God, I can't wait to get back and sleep. I just want to chill, you know? I just want this to be over so we can—"

And then I saw her. Standing right there in the middle of the crowd. Cheyenne was not dead. She was there. And she was staring right at me. Her blunt-cut blond hair. Her blue eyes. Her perfect skin. Her big diamond earrings. Definitely her.

"Josh!" I gasped, gripping his hand.

"What? What's the matter?"

"Cheyenne," I told him, breathless. A crowd of men in dark suits moved in between myself and Cheyenne, and when they moved away again, she was gone. I scanned the crowd like a crazy person, but she had disappeared. Was she a figment of my imagination?

"Cheyenne what?" Josh asked. "Reed, take a breath."

I did as I was told, and my brain cleared a bit. A figment of my imagination. Of course she had been. Cheyenne was dead. Her parents had just sent her ashes into the wind. I was just tired. Just imagining things.

"What is it?" Josh asked again as I clutched his hand.

"Nothing. I just . . ." I glanced up at him and forced a strained laugh. "You're gonna think I'm crazy. I seriously just thought I saw Cheyenne."

Josh blinked. "Oh. Okay, I could see why that would freak you out," he said with an understanding smile, briefly cupping my cheek. "You probably just saw one of her cousins or something. Someone who looks like her."

I looked into his eyes and my panic dissipated. A cousin. Right. Someone who looked like her. Of course. I wasn't crazy. I'd merely spotted a look-alike. What would I do without him?

"Okay?" he asked, loosening his grip a bit.

I nodded. "Okay.

"You're sleeping in the car on the way home," he told me, slipping his arm around my waist as we started walking again.

"Like Gage and Trey are gonna let me sleep," I said with a forced laugh.

"I'll kick them out. You can sack out in the backseat," he told me.

"How're they gonna get home?" I asked.

"They'll find a ride. Everyone we know is here. All I care about is you," he added with a smile.

God, he was perfect. What had I been thinking, flirting with a hot billionaire real estate heir? Did I really need to create drama in my life when it seemed to have a way of finding me quite easily on its own? Answer? An emphatic *no*. I tipped my head to the side and rested it on Josh's strong shoulder as we made our way down the beach to his car.

I loved him. I did. Him and only him. From this moment on.

POWER

"It's like a morgue in here," Astrid said that evening, hugging her purple sweater closer to her body. She shivered and sat down next to me on the settee in the foyer. Sabine leaned against the wall under the framed photos of illustrious Billings alumni, many of whom had been present that morning to pay their respects to their lost sister. In the parlor most of our fellow Billings Girls sat in pensive silence. The TV was on, but I was sure no one was paying attention to it. In the hour we'd been back on campus, not one person had even approached Cheyenne's room to take her parents up on their generous, if morbid, offer. "So much for that whole moving on thing."

"Give it time," I said. "We did just scatter her ashes this morning."

The moment we'd returned I'd run directly up to my room and stuffed the photo Cheyenne's mother had given me into one of my textbooks from last year, then shoved it in the very bottom of the bottom drawer of my desk. Out of sight, out of mind. Except that it wasn't, since it kept flashing across my mind's eye every other second. Yeah, moving on was not going to be easy. Especially not for me.

"My mum always says death is a natural part of life," Astrid said, looking down at her black-and-white checkered shoes. I noticed she had picked off most of her bright yellow nail polish and had eschewed her usual glitter eye shadow today, going for a more subdued gray. "But this doesn't feel natural, does it?"

"That's because it's not. It's not natural when it's suicide," I said glumly.

"We have to do something," Sabine said suddenly, pushing herself away from the wall. Being a true island girl, she owned no black clothing, and she looked awkward in my black skirt and gray top. Like she was a little girl playing librarian or something. "It's too depressing."

Astrid and I glanced at each other. "Like what?" I asked.

"I don't know. Something," Sabine said, pacing in front of us. "All of us together. Like you've said you all did last year. Something to cheer us up and help us to . . . you know . . . what's the word?"

"Bond?" I suggested.

"Yes! *Exactement!*" Sabine's eyes were bright with excitement.

"But what could we do?" Astrid asked, sitting up straight.

"I'm not sure. Reed, you know these girls better than we do," Sabine pointed out. "What would they all like to do?"

"I don't know . . . shop?" I joked. It was, after all, the universal Billings Girl pastime.

"Brilliant!" Astrid said.

"Yes! That's it!" Sabine added, clasping her hands together and pointing her index fingers at me. "Shopping. We should all go shopping together!"

I blinked up at her. I'd been kidding, after all. I mean, was this really an appropriate moment for shameless acts of consumerism?

"You think?" I said.

"Definitely!" Sabine replied, pulling me up off the settee. "It's a perfect idea, Reed."

A spark of something akin to excitement filled my chest. It would be so nice to do something normal. Something distracting. Something fun. The last few weeks had been so bleak, a few hours off from that would be such a relief.

"Well, we do have a free pass off campus all weekend. . . ."

Normally anything but flexible, Headmaster Cromwell had granted us all the passes because of the memorial service, knowing some families would be around and that some students would likely stay up at the Cape overnight. I suppose he assumed it would be easier just to give everyone a universal "get out of jail free" card than to deal with people coming in and filing requests every other second.

"Good! You should go tell them. Cheer them up," Sabine said, pointing at the parlor.

She and Astrid both looked so stoked by the idea, I could hardly say no. I walked over to the parlor door and peeked in. The other Billings Girls were all sitting on the U of couches, staring into space or whispering to each other. London twirled her hair around her finger, then let it go, then twirled it again. Portia toyed idly with her necklaces. Constance texted on her phone, undoubtedly to Whittaker. Other than the occasional whisper and the sound of her fingers punching the keys, the room was fairly silent.

"You guys? We kind of had an idea we wanted to run by you," I began.

I had their attention instantly.

"It was really Reed's idea," Sabine said, coming up behind me.

"I was thinking maybe tomorrow we could all go shopping," I suggested. "Walk into town . . . hit those cute shops on Main Street? Maybe we could even have lunch at the Driscoll."

"Really?"

London and Vienna popped up like those moles in the Whack-a-Mole games at the Jersey Shore. The whispering intensified into excited murmurs.

"I am totally in," Portia said. "I am the Q of retail therapy."

A few people laughed and the murmurs turned to chatter. Who needed what? Who was going to burn out Daddy's credit card first? The morgue had suddenly morphed into a cocktail party. Without the cocktails, of course.

"This was a fab idea, Reed," Portia said, double air-kissing me. "I'm going to go do a shoe inventory right now."

Tiffany, Rose, London, Vienna, Kiki, and Lorna were all smiling at me, and I suddenly felt an enormous sense of satisfaction. Felt very Noelle Lange. I had taken charge. I had just completely changed the vibe from depths of despair to excited anticipation in about two seconds flat.

Later that night everyone but me had been to Cheyenne's room. Shelby was the first to tentatively approach, but once the seal had been broken, all the other Billings Girls had been through there, whispering like they were in a museum. Only I stayed in my room, alone. I knew Cheyenne wouldn't want me to have anything of hers, and the last thing I needed was some token to remind me of my guilt each time I saw it. Finally, when they were all done, I heard everyone adjourn to the parlor to hang out, but I didn't join them. I felt heavy. Like I couldn't move. Bed was the only place I wanted to be.

I have no idea how long I lay there, staring at the ceiling—brooding about everything that had happened that day—but when the door opened, I sat up, more than ready for a distraction. Sabine struggled in with a large box covered in airmail stamps. She paused when she saw me.

"Oh. I thought you were downstairs with everyone else," she said.

"Nope. What's that?" I asked, gesturing at the box.

"Care package from home," she said, dropping it on the floor of her closet. "I left it downstairs before."

"Cool. Aren't you going to open it?" I asked as she closed the closet door.

"Maybe later. My mother always puts in these sentimental notes and cards," she said, pushing her hands into the back pockets of her jeans. "I'm sort of not in the mood."

I could understand that. There had already been way too much emotional spillage around here today.

"What did you take from Cheyenne's?" I asked.

"Nothing," Sabine said, picking at some unseen speck on the back of her desk chair. "I don't want anything of hers." Then she pulled a small pink jewelry box from the pocket of her jeans. "Tiffany made me take this, though. She made Constance, Lorna, and me all take them."

She cracked the box open. Inside was a very familiar diamond *B* on a gold chain. My heart thumped extra hard when I saw it: the symbol of Billings membership Cheyenne had given to each of us at the beginning of the year, but had withheld from Sabine, Constance, and Lorna—the girls she had deemed unworthy. Tiffany must have found them in her room. I hadn't worn mine in days. Thinking about it now, I realized I hadn't seen any of the Billings Girls wearing them. When had they stopped?

"Are you going to wear it?" I asked.

"No." She snapped the box closed and tossed it unceremoniously on her desk. "Diamonds are so tacky," she joked, smiling wanly.

I exhaled a laugh. For a long moment neither of us said a word.

"Do you want to . . . I don't know . . . play cards or something?" I asked finally.

Sabine's green eyes lit up. "Definitely!"

She came over and bounced down on my bed as I fished a deck of cards from my top desk drawer. From that moment on it was all Spit and Rummy and Go Fish, which Sabine had never played. Neither of us mentioned Cheyenne again, and for a couple of hours I actually felt close to normal. Not completely. But close.

BEST IDEA EVER

"You *must* let me buy it for you, Reed," Portia said. "It is so you."

It was a gorgeous dress. A red Nicole Miller, sleeveless and slim, with a skirt that hit just above the knee and a sophisticated boat neck. It accentuated my long legs and defined arms, and was sexy without being slutty. Kind of a perfect Billings Girl dress. It had been a long time since I'd felt anything this luxurious touch my skin. Not since I'd gotten rid of all the stuff Noelle and the others had given me last year. I'd even trashed that frothy, shimmery gold gown they'd chosen for me to wear to the Legacy—perhaps the only move I regretted. I had felt so beautiful that night. So . . . not me. Sort of how I felt looking at myself right now.

Part of me would have loved to have just said, "Sure, Portia. Ring it up." But it was a six-hundred-dollar dress. And also red. A little bit "look at me!" for my taste.

"It's too expensive," I told Portia, checking my reflection from the side.

"BFD. Besides, 'expensive' is a relative term," Portia said with a sniff.

Ew.

"I wasn't expecting to buy anything. I only tried it on for fun."

"Isn't that what this day is supposed to be all about? Fun?" Tiffany asked, leaning back in the large dressing room to snap my picture. She was wearing a silver minidress with a halter collar. Her appearance would have caused accidents on any major freeway in America. "Let the girl buy it for you. She has money coming out of her—"

"Don't finish that sentence!" Portia demanded, throwing up a hand. "Like I really need the visual of money coming out any of my orifices. Why do people think that's amusing?"

She forcibly turned me to the side and undid the zipper. "Take it off. We're putting it on the card. What's another six bills gonna matter anyway? Look at my pile."

I looked. Sweaters, skirts, scarves, dresses. The pile was the size of a VW Bug.

"Well, maybe. But if I'm going to get it, I'm going to get the green one," I said.

"Uh, no. Green is my color," Portia said.

"Excuse me?" I asked.

"Green. It's my signature color," she replied, blithely fluffing her hair in the mirror. She did, come to think of it, wear a lot of green. "I'm only buying it if it's the red."

Tiffany and I looked at each other and laughed. "Guess the fairy godmother gets to pick out the clothes," Tiffany joked, earning a scathing look from Portia, which she ignored. "But you should get it anyway, Reed. Red is a good color for you. It's a power color."

A power color. Huh. I looked at my reflection again. It did sort of highlight my brown hair and still semitanned skin. If red was a power color, maybe I should get used to wearing it. That was the whole point of being at Easton, after all. To break out of the Croton, Pennsylvania, rut and live life the way these girls lived it. Live life as someone who was going somewhere. Someone who got noticed.

"Come on, Reed. Decision time," Portia said, flicking out her American Express Black and holding it up between two fingers. "This offer expires in five . . . four . . . three . . . two—"

"Okay! Okay, I'll take it," I said. "But I owe you one."

I stepped out of the dress and added it to Portia's pile on the bench, then pulled my jeans and sweater back on.

Portia smirked. "Great. Can't wait to see how you pay me back."

I wasn't sure if that was a dig or not—or maybe a threat, considering all the not-so-pleasant things I'd had to do for the Billings Girls in the past—but I didn't get a chance to ask. London and Vienna chose that moment to barrel into our room all flushed with excitement, their arms full of clothes.

"What're you guys getting?" London asked, eyeing Portia's armful.

"Just a few things," Portia said. "It's really too bad about the Legacy. They have some gorge gowns in that back room."

"I know. God. Halloween is going to be such a downer this year," London pouted. "I'm totally wearing my gown anyway. I'll wear it to class if I have to."

Just like that, an idea hit me like a smack to the head. An idea so obvious I was shocked it hadn't occurred to anyone before now. The perfect way to give the Billings Girls what they wanted, but to do it in a totally unshallow, socially acceptable way. "What if we had our own masquerade party?" I asked.

"What do you mean?" Portia asked.

"I mean, if the Legacy isn't going to happen, maybe Billings should throw its own masquerade ball," I said. "It would just be Easton students, but it would be something to do. And someplace to wear your gowns."

"Interesting," Tiffany murmured, her bottom lip protruding.

"Wait a minute. I thought you were all 'how can we party when Cheyenne SFU,'" Portia said, unburdening herself of her clothing pile again. "What's with the one-eighty?"

"Well, I was thinking we could do it as a fund-raiser in Cheyenne's name," I suggested. "We can establish a scholarship in her honor and sell tickets to the ball. All the proceeds could go into the scholarship fund."

"The Cheyenne Martin Scholarship Fund!" Vienne cheered, bouncing up and down as she clapped her hands.

"Oooh. I like that idea!" Tiffany said.

"Like it? It's effing brill," Portia said. "And now I can go try on gowns!"

Portia gave me a double air-kiss before twirling out of the room. Tiffany patted me on the back and London and Vienna whipped me up in a three-way hug.

"Reed, you are totally my savior!" Vienna said.

"Best idea ever," London agreed.

They all ran out of the room on Portia's heels, knocking on dressing room doors and spreading the news to the other girls. I was left behind to revel in my moment of glory. It *was* a good idea. And it felt good to be doing something in Cheyenne's name. Something she never would have expected me to do. Like maybe I was proving her wrong about me somehow.

"Reed! I just heard about the fund-raiser! What an incredible thought! Her parents are going to freak!" Constance rambled, bounding into my room with Sabine on her heels.

"Definitely. It's absolutely perfect," Sabine added.

"Yeah, go you," Missy grumbled as she walked by. "Like no one's ever created a scholarship fund before."

I rolled my eyes and ignored her, choosing to bask in the glow of praise. I just hoped that my new red dress would be special enough for the party. But then, I was the one throwing it, wasn't I? For once I was going to be able to set the standard. I looked at my reflection in the mirror and smiled. I really felt like a whole new Reed.

LADIES WHO LUNCH

The restaurant at the Driscoll Hotel was all old-world elegance. Gleaming oak tables, gold fleur-de-lis wallpaper, gleaming crystal stemware, white linen napkins, sun-streaked windows overlooking a beautiful pond where actual swans cut sleek lines across the smooth surface. It was the type of place that would have made a girl in jeans and boots feel out of place . . . if she hadn't been surrounded by fourteen of the most impeccably dressed and groomed girls on the East Coast.

The atmosphere at the table was convivial as we all chatted over finger sandwiches and iced tea. My Billings Masquerade idea had upped everyone's moods considerably, and all anyone could talk about was where it should be held, who should be invited, and who might need to be paid off to keep the liquor flowing and the authorities at bay. I hadn't heard this much laughter in days.

"Nice work, Reed," Sabine whispered in my ear as she refolded her napkin in her lap.

"What do you mean?" I asked.

She draped her arm over the back of my chair and leaned in. "Look around. Your day trip plan definitely worked. No one here looks depressed about Cheyenne."

My heart contracted at the sound of her name, but I let it pass. She was right. Everyone was clearly starting to move on. Mrs. Kane would be so pleased.

Tiffany stood up, tapping her fork against her glass. Everyone instantly fell silent and looked up at her expectantly.

"I'd like to make a toast," Tiffany said, lifting her glass. "To our friend Cheyenne."

Heart squeeze.

"We'll miss you. And we hope that wherever you are, you're happier than you were here."

Tiffany raised her glass higher and everyone did the same.

"To Cheyenne."

We all clinked and everyone fell silent for a moment, each thinking her own private thoughts. I just hoped Cheyenne was, in fact, out there somewhere and that she would appreciate our gesture in her name. That it might somehow make things right. Finally, London stood and cleared her throat.

"There's a . . . a . . . what is it? A point of business we need to take care of!" she announced, seeming pleased that she'd used such an important-sounding phrase. "Billings needs a president. I think we should elect one now."

"Is that really appropriate?" Missy asked, her face screwing up in consternation. If she wasn't careful, she was really going to give herself premature wrinkles. "Cheyenne's only been gone a week."

A few people murmured their agreement.

"Yeah, and if she were here with us now, I think she'd say that Billings needs a leader," Vienna put in, standing next to London. They looked as Twin Cities as ever, one in a purple knit minidress, the other in a black knit minidress, and each with a colorful scarf holding back her teased hair. "Besides, we all know who it's going to be. What's the point in putting off the inevitable?"

Wait. *We all know who it's going to be?* Who? I didn't know. I looked up, curious, and saw that everyone aside from Missy was staring at me.

I pushed back from the table, overcome by a sudden wave of extreme heat. "What? No way."

"Are you saying you don't *want* to be president of Billings?" Portia demanded. Like the very idea was just unimaginable.

"No, I'm not. I just . . . why me?" I asked, flabbergasted.

"Reed, it's totally obvious," Rose said gently, leaning into the table so I could see her. "Look at all you've done this year. You were the only one who stood up to Cheyenne during initiation—"

"You've shown everyone here what it really means to be a strong Billings role model," Tiffany confirmed. "You stood up for what you believed in, even when all your sisters didn't agree."

"You stood up for us," Lorna clarified, earning an irritated look from Missy.

"And then coming up with this retail therapy idea . . . and the masquerade and scholarship fund," Rose said. "All you."

"You're already our leader. It's just not official yet," Astrid said.

"Besides, you're a junior, so you can hold the post for two years," Tiffany added, lifting her camera to snap my picture and preserve my stunned expression for posterity. "If there's one thing Billings needs right now, it's a little stability."

My palms were sweating in my lap. I didn't deserve this. I didn't. Cheyenne would still have been there if it wasn't for me. Or so she said. I couldn't take her place. Could I?

"I don't know what to say," I blurted.

"You don't have to say anything," Tiffany replied. "All in favor of Reed Brennan for president?" she said.

"Aye!" came the general reply. They all raised their hands. All fourteen of them. Even the ever-silent Shelby Wordsworth. Even Missy, though her hand didn't make it quite as high as the others.

Everyone applauded politely so as to not disturb the other ladies-who-lunch, and suddenly I couldn't stop smiling. I felt so honored. So stunned. So floored that they would want me. That they would *all* want me.

This was just what I needed. A united house. The confidence of my friends. A real new beginning.

Reed Brennan. President of Billings House.

DESERVED

We barely fit through the front door of Billings with all our bags and packages. Everyone was talking jovially, reviewing their purchases, striking deals over who could borrow what from whom. Clearly retail therapy was a legitimate method of treatment for depression. At least inside the circle.

"Reed, you have to stop by and try on that red dress for us again," Shelby demanded. Perhaps the first words she'd ever spoken to me unbidden. Not that I was feeling bitter toward her right then. Right then I was loving everyone. "I think I have a pair of Louboutins that would go perfectly."

"The strappies with the gold? Totally!" Portia agreed.

"Why don't we all go back to my room now and we can all show everyone what we bought?" I suggested, not wanting the party to end. I was too high on this freedom from guilt I was feeling. Wanted to keep it at bay. And bonding with the girls was fun. It had been so long since we'd allowed ourselves to have fun.

"Fashion show!" Vienna and London sang, throwing their arms up.

"Fab idea," Portia said happily.

I laughed and turned to Sabine. "Okay, is it just me, or is everyone suddenly my best friend?" I whispered.

"This is what happens to women in power," Sabine replied with a laugh, reaching out to squeeze my hand. "Get used to it. You deserve it."

My chest swelled with pride, even though it seemed ridiculous that anyone might think I deserved this. But if that was what they really felt, I wasn't about to argue with them. I just wanted to hold on to this. I just wanted to feel this good for as long as possible.

We all tromped up the stairs to the top floor together, a mass of flipping hair, swinging shopping bags, and laughter. I was just about to turn and open the door to my room when someone stepped out into the hallway. Stepped out into the hallway from Cheyenne's room.

"There you are! I've been waiting for *hours* for someone to get back here and help me unpack all my shit!"

We all stopped short, slamming into one another, tripping forward. The laughter died. There was no way I was seeing who I thought I was seeing. But there she was. Thick brown hair. Imperious chin. That mischievous glimmer in her eyes.

Noelle Lange was back.

SURPRISE

"Noelle! Oh my God! What are you doing here?"

After they recovered from their shock, everyone rushed forward, shrieking and shouting questions. Noelle was engulfed by the crowd as they all tried to hug her at once, their bony elbows and designer watches banging together. I, however, was rooted to the spot. As were the rest of the juniors. Constance, Sabine, Astrid, Kiki, Missy, and Lorna. They didn't know Noelle. In fact, most of them probably feared her. But that wasn't why I wasn't moving. I was simply too stunned to control my motor functions.

How could she not have told me she was coming back? I'd seen her just last weekend. She had to have known. But she had acted aloof, mentioning all the places she wanted to travel to now that she was off probation. Had she wanted to surprise me, or was this another one of her games? God, I hoped it was the former.

Finally, the crowd around Noelle thinned out a bit and she looked right at me. Looked right at me and smirked.

"Surprise!" she said.

She moved forward through the throng, walked right up to me, and hugged me. It was a real, firm, full-body hug. Not one of those stiff things you give someone you're supposed to like but don't. Her signature scent enveloped me, that slightly spicy, slightly flowery perfume she'd worn for as long as I'd known her. I instantly relaxed.

"Noelle. Why didn't you—"

"Tell you? And miss the look on your face right now? Please," Noelle said, flipping her hair over her shoulder. "A girl likes to have her fun."

The seniors chuckled knowingly. The juniors shifted in discomfort. I couldn't have torn my eyes away from Noelle if I'd tried.

She reached for my hands and spoke in an intimate tone, as if no one else was there. "You're finally going to see Billings the way it's supposed to be."

There was a lump in my throat the size of a soccer ball. How did she know exactly what I wanted to hear? Now that she was back—back where she belonged—Billings was Billings again.

Noelle's eyes slid past my shoulder. "Do I know you?"

I glanced behind me just as Sabine replied, "No. I don't think so."

"Noelle Lange, this is Sabine DuLac," I said, lifting a hand in introduction. "She's a transfer this year."

"A pleasure," Noelle said with a small smile.

"I've heard so much about you," Sabine gushed.

"Really? I've heard nothing about you," Noelle replied, looking bored as she picked an invisible piece of lint off her Chaiken sweater.

Sabine's excited expression crumbled and she shot me a betrayed and embarrassed look. I wanted to explain that I would have told Noelle all about her if I'd had any contact with the girl whatsoever before last weekend. But it seemed too lame to try to explain right then in front of everyone, and people were starting to chatter again, asking Noelle where she'd been and whether she'd heard from Kiran Hayes or Taylor Bell and what was up with her and Dash. Questions I was dying to hear the answers to.

"Come on, Reed. I've got some presents for you," Noelle said over her shoulder, as the others ushered her toward her room.

Presents? This just got better and better. I shot Sabine an apologetic look, resolved to explain later, and followed Noelle. Just like old times.

THE FUTURE OF BILLINGS

"So, what *is* up with you and Dash?" Shelby asked as Noelle flipped open the top of her Louis Vuitton trunk.

I held my breath as she stood up straight. She shot a conspiratorial look over her shoulder. "Dash is fine," she said, deftly avoiding the real question. Did she not want our friends to know they'd broken up? And if not, why? "Have you heard he was the only freshman at Yale to make the sailing team?"

As the other girls "oohed" and "ahhed" over this achievement, my insides burned. How did she know this and I didn't? She was supposed to be broken up with him, and he'd been e-mailing me since the beginning of the year. Maybe I wasn't worthy of the big news. Not like Noelle.

"So, this Cromwell guy is kind of a jackass, huh?" Noelle said, tossing an armful of cashmere sweaters and scarves from the trunk into a drawer and slamming it shut. For a girl who owned some of the most expensive stuff available to womankind, she had never treated any of it with all that much respect. To her, everything was replaceable, expendable. She had an endless supply of luxury at her fingertips.

London, Vienna, Tiffany, Portia, Rose, Shelby, and I were all gathered around the room, but none of us dared answer. Everyone was clearly a tad freaked at being back in Cheyenne's room now that her parents had cleaned it out. They must have come and gone while we were shopping. It seemed so empty, even with Noelle's bags piled everywhere. So eerie. I couldn't speak for anyone else, but I had this creepy feeling that someone was watching us. Judging us.

"What?" Noelle asked, noting the silence.

"We hate him," London blurted.

"That's an understatement," Portia said.

"He killed Cheyenne," Vienna put in.

Whiplash. "What?" I steadied myself against Cheyenne's—no, Noelle's—desk.

"Everyone knows it," London said, her eyes wide. "He expelled her, then she killed herself that night. We all know she, like, lived for this place. Ergo—"

"Everyone here blames him," Tiffany said, adjusting the long lens on her old-school camera.

How did I not know this? Maybe because I'd been too busy obsessing about who Cheyenne herself had blamed.

"If he hadn't been such an unyielding asshole—"

"Tell me about it," Noelle said, rolling her eyes. "My dad had to threaten to close this place down before he let me back in."

"Close down Easton? Could your dad do that?" I asked, although it wouldn't really surprise me.

"Not in so many words. But he could sue . . . and sue . . . and sue," Noelle said with a laugh. "And trust me, Daddy's pockets are far deeper than Easton's. Eventually, this place would have crumbled. Once Cromwell understood that fact, he caved like a cheap wedding tent."

"Wow. He must be PO'd," Portia said, perching on the edge of the single bed. Cheyenne's parents had removed all her custom furniture, so now the standard-issue Billings stuff was back. At least until Noelle redecorated.

"Oh, he is. Believe me," Noelle said, tossing her iPod on the desk. "Have you guys seen how he gets all shaky when he's angry? It's very Frankenstein's monster."

Everyone laughed, but Noelle scrunched her nose and ran her finger across the surface of the desk. "What's this? Did you guys hold a Studio 54 party in here?" Her fingertip was caked in some kind of thick white dust.

"That's probably left over from when the police dusted for fingerprints," Tiffany said, staring at Noelle's finger. "The desk is the only piece of Billings furniture Cheyenne was using, so . . ."

Noelle's jaw dropped as she looked around at us. "They dusted for prints? Why? I thought it was suicide."

"It was," Rose said quietly, staring out the bay window. "They just . . ."

"Wanted to make sure," I finished, swallowing hard.

"Guess they're a tad suspicious when it comes to Easton," Portia said wryly.

Noelle's expression darkened. She looked toward the opposite side of the room. The side of the room that had once belonged to Ariana Osgood. To her best friend. To the girl who had turned out to be a cold-blooded killer.

"Gee. I wonder why," Noelle said.

For a moment no one spoke, but then Noelle slapped her hands together to clear away the dust.

"So. What else is going on around here?" she asked, dumping the contents of her massive cosmetics bag into the top drawer of the desk. "I mean, aside from this Driscoll Dinner thing that Cromwell kept spewing about at our meeting."

The Driscoll Alumni Dinner. Right. I had completely forgotten about it in all the drama. The dinner was to be held at the Driscoll Hotel this Saturday, the central event of alumni weekend. Every student had been required to join a committee to help plan or work at the event. Sabine and I were going to be servers. I felt a skitter of nerves down my spine as I wondered for the millionth time if Dash was planning on attending, but I quickly and guiltily banished the thought, as if Noelle could read my mind.

"Oh my God! We're getting a Coffee Carma!" Vienna announced, bubbling up the mood considerably.

"Oh, yeah. Amberly is a freshman this year. I totally forgot. I'll have to go say hi before my mother calls me and starts badgering me to," Noelle said.

"Right. You guys know each other," I said.

"Oh, so you've met our little Amberly." Noelle was amused.

"She gave Reed a Carma Card," London said petulantly.

"Not surprising. I've told her all about Billings and you in particular, Reed," Noelle said. "She must be laying the groundwork. Smart girl."

Noelle placed a jewelry box on the dresser. "What else?"

"Well, you heard about the Legacy, obvi," Portia said, flinging her glossy black hair over her shoulder.

"Yeah. That's such a crock," Noelle said, sifting through her makeup. She selected a tube of M.A.C. lip gloss and opened it. "Someone will step up and throw the thing. Believe me, one unfortunate incident will not stop the Legacy."

"You think?" London asked hopefully.

"I know," Noelle replied, whipping open a gold compact mirror and touching up her bottom lip.

"Well, just in case, Reed came up with an alternate plan," Tiffany said.

"A fabulous alternate plan," Rose added.

Noelle raised one eyebrow, her lip gloss wand pausing just millimeters from her top lip. "And what's that?

"We're going to throw our own Halloween masquerade!" Vienna exclaimed.

"In Cheyenne's honor," Shelby added.

I watched Noelle expectantly. Hopefully. I wanted her approval. Even after all this time.

"Really?" Noelle continued with her makeup application. "How very industrious of you, Reed. Look at you, taking all the initiative. I'd say, 'You go, girl,' but it's just so passé."

I smiled and shook my head. That was about right. That was about as much praise as I was ever going to receive from her. But still, it felt good.

"And Reed's our new president!" London said, coming over to fling her arm around me.

Noelle snapped the compact closed. My chest instantly tightened with dread. The look on her face was unreadable. Anger? Shock? Both? I felt myself backpedaling like mad. I didn't want to step on her toes. She was Noelle Lange. Who was I to be president of Billings if Noelle Lange was here?

"Well, well," Noelle said, crossing her arms over her chest as she eyed me. "Glass-Licker's come a long way."

"Well, I mean . . . now that you're back, things are different," I stammered. "Obviously you're the one who should be . . . I mean, if you'd been here, there's no way I would have been elected."

Noelle simply looked at me. Nobody argued my point. *Thanks for the support, girls.* So much for them thinking I was the patent choice. Although I couldn't really blame them. This was Noelle. Even I knew she should be president.

I cleared my throat. If I was going to do this, if I was going to give up the coveted presidency so soon after winning it, I was going to do it with some dignity. Not like a stammering idiot.

"This place was not the same without you," I said evenly. "It's always felt like your house to me. So if you want the presidency, it's all yours."

Everyone looked at Noelle. I tucked my hands into my back pockets and held my breath. Slowly, her lips turned up in a smile. "That's sweet of you, Reed, really, but no thanks."

I blinked, stunned. Relieved, but stunned.

"What?" Portia blurted, voicing the word bubble hanging above all our heads.

Noelle shrugged and tossed the lip gloss back in the drawer. "Look, technically, I shouldn't even be here. I should have graduated last year, but, well, things happen. I'm only here to prove to the Ivies that I want to do the work. That I don't expect special treatment."

The incredulity was obvious on my friends' faces. Noelle didn't expect special treatment? She had never known life without it. Even among the most privileged girls in the country, she was privileged. And she never let anyone forget it.

"You're the future of this place, Reed," Noelle said, turning to face me. "All I want is to make sure that when I do finally leave here, I leave it in good hands. And I couldn't imagine better hands than yours."

Whoa. Everyone looked at me, impressed. Now *that* was praise. Even though the girls of Billings had voted me in, even though the vote had been unanimous, this was true validation.

"Thanks, Noelle," I said warmly.

"You're welcome." She smiled, an unreadable—maybe teasing?—glint in her eye. "Madame President."

JOSH'S MANTRA

The next morning at breakfast, Josh picked up a coffee cup and slammed it onto his tray. He held a bowl under the cereal dispenser and jammed down on the lever. I heard a crack, and was surprised when the plastic handle didn't break off. When the bowl overflowed with Apple Jacks, he cursed under his breath, grabbed a handful of cereal, and tossed it toward the garbage can behind the counter. Little orange and green Os rained everywhere. I think only one hit the actual can.

All around us, students studiously avoided the topic of Cheyenne and her memorial service, and instead buzzed about alumni weekend, coming up at the end of the week. They chatted about what they would wear, about which illustrious graduates might attend, about how best to sneak alcohol out of the Driscoll Hotel on Saturday night. But it was clear that Josh and I would not be participating in such frivolous banter.

"My woman's intuition is telling me something's bothering you," I joked, trying to lighten his mood.

He looked at me like I was the enemy. "I can't believe she's back. How the hell could they let her back in?"

I took a deep breath. Noelle. Of course. What else could possibly be bothering him? But I had to remind myself that he had good reason to hate her. She had been all too ready to pin Thomas's murder on him last year, even though she had suspected all along that it had been Ariana. And even if Josh had never been arrested, he would have been totally justified in hating her simply for the role she'd played in his best friend's death. She, Kiran, Taylor, and Ariana had kidnapped Thomas from his room and brought him out to the woods, where they had tied him up and basically left him scared and alone. All to teach him a lesson. All to make him feel as helpless and humiliated as he'd made me feel the evening before at a party in the woods. What they had done was awful, but it had been Ariana who had gone back and murdered him. The others hadn't known of her sadistic jaunt. In my opinion, Noelle and the others had messed up big-time, but they hadn't intended for Thomas to die. They had simply thought they were playing a prank. That was the way I justified it. The only logic that helped me sleep at night.

"Well, apparently her parents threatened to sue and that was that," I said calmly, adding a bagel to my tray. I pushed up the sleeves of the black V-neck cashmere sweater Noelle had given me—one of many gifts, which included Miu Miu boots, a Tiffany monogrammed lock necklace, and an iPhone—hoping he wouldn't ask me where it had come from. She'd said she was making up for the fact that she'd missed my birthday last year. And Christmas. And something about Flag Day.

"Shocker. Gotta love America. They should rename the country Litigation Nation," he grumbled. He took a deep breath and blew it out through his nose, placing his hands on his hips. "You have to get out of Billings now. With her back, it's going to be just like it was last year."

"No. It's not," I replied.

"Really? How do you figure?" he asked.

"Well, for one, I'm in charge," I told him. "They elected me president, remember? Which, by the way, you haven't even congratulated me on."

Josh exhaled audibly and gave me a sheepish look. "You're right. I'm sorry. Congratulations. At least they got something right over there."

"Thank you," I said with a nod. It was the highest praise my Billings sisters were going to get from him. "So Noelle is not going to be running things this year. I am."

"Yeah, right," Josh said, picking up his tray and turning toward the cafeteria.

My face stung. Did he not realize how insulting that was? "Thanks a lot," I said, following after him.

Josh looked at me and his expression softened. "I'm sorry. I didn't mean it that way." He shrugged, gripping his full tray with both hands. "It's just . . . I know that girl. She's not happy unless she's surrounded by drama and scandal. Come on. Just transfer to Pemberly or something. It's not that big of a deal. And at least it'll get you away from her."

"Not that big a deal? I can't just transfer after they elected me!" My skin burned. "And do I have to remind you that Noelle saved my life last year?"

"No. But it wouldn't have even been in jeopardy if it hadn't been for her and her morally suspect Billings friends," Josh replied. "Why can't you see what a cancer that place is?"

"God, Josh. Enough already with the 'death to Billings' riff," I snapped. "That's like your new mantra."

He pulled his head back, surprised, and his brow furrowed. "I'm only thinking of you."

"Yeah, well, I can handle myself, thanks."

I turned and stormed away, taking a seat at the opposite end of the table from where we usually sat. He followed after me slowly and, taking my cue, grabbed a seat with Trey at a separate table. As I rather violently shook up my bottle of orange juice, a couple of girls from the freshman soccer team strolled by with their food.

"Hi, Reed," one of them said. "Congratulations on the Billings presidency."

"Totally. Congrats," the other echoed. "I *love* your sweater, by the way."

"Thanks," I said, completely caught off guard. I'd never spoken to either of these girls before. Didn't even know their names. How had they heard about the Billings vote?

"Listen, my dad works for the New England Revolution and he can get us on the sidelines when they play the Galaxy next spring. We're totally going to meet Becks. Wanna come?" the first girl babbled.

I blinked. That was a lot of information. And a seriously sick offer—meeting all those pro players. "Um, who could turn down a sideline pass?" I said. "What's your name again?"

The girl blushed, but gamely answered, "I'm Ava Greene. And this is Demetria Wallace."

"Thanks, Ava," I said. "That's very cool of you."

"I'm just so glad you're in!" Ava replied. "Well, see you at practice!" They strode off together, their heads bent close as they gabbed.

"Yeah. See ya," I replied to thin air.

Okay. That was bizarre. But I guess being president of Billings came with perks I hadn't even thought of.

I glanced over at Josh as I reached for my bagel, wondering if he'd noticed. He chewed mechanically on a doughnut, staring straight ahead and looking morose. I felt a pang of both sorrow and irritation in my chest. I loved that he cared. I really did. But I was starting to wonder if there was such a thing as caring too much.

SUZEL

"Did you know that George Washington didn't want to be president?" Sabine asked me that night. She turned around in her desk chair, all excited, the seashell bangles she always wore clicking together. American history was her antidrug. She was learning it for the first time, coming from a foreign land and all, and each new fact got her all starry-eyed—like the rest of Billings got whenever they heard Stella McCartney was coming out with a new line or that Jake Gyllenhaal was shirtless in some new magazine. It was kind of cool, actually, seeing someone get all fizzy about stuff I'd known since grade school.

I placed my pencil down on my calculus notebook and flexed my aching fingers. Apparently I'd been gripping the thing too hard. A callus was starting to form on the inside of my middle finger.

"Yeah, I do remember that," I said. "He didn't think he was worthy or something, right?"

"Kind of like you," Sabine teased.

I looked down at my pencil-dented fingers. "I think I'm worthy," I lied.

"Just that Noelle is more worthy," she said perceptively.

My cheeks reddened. "Yeah, well, she's just . . . Noelle. You'd get it if you knew her."

Sabine's face fell and she quickly turned back to her work. "Well, I don't."

And thanks for reminding me, her tone said. But how was I supposed to explain it? How was I supposed to convey what it had been like for me last fall? I could hardly define it myself. I had worshipped Noelle. Hated her. Loved her. Feared her. Needed her. There was no way to quantify Noelle's . . . Noelle-ness. It was something you had to experience for yourself.

"Sabine, I—"

A knock at our door cut me off. We both looked at it, perplexed. No one ever knocked. They just barreled right in, usually with some hair crisis or vital gossip already spewing forth before the door had even slammed shut.

"Come in?" I said tentatively.

Noelle opened the door and stepped back to allow a distinguished-looking middle-aged woman to step inside. She was wearing a gorgeously cut power suit and a thick gold necklace, and had perfect blond highlights that even Ariana would have died for. In her hands was a large, silver-wrapped gift with a thick, silky red bow. Her smile was warm and genuine, but something about the way she carried herself was all business. Even though she was tiny, her presence somehow filled up the room. I stood up, feeling instinctively that it was the right thing to do.

"Ladies, so sorry to interrupt your study session," the woman said, with a slight Southern accent.

"Oh, it's no problem," I answered quickly.

"Reed Brennan, I'd like you to meet Susan Llewelyn," Noelle said cordially. "Suzel is head of the Billings alumni committee as well as a member of the Easton Academy board of directors."

"A pleasure to meet you, Reed," Suzel said, stepping forward to hand me the large, heavy box. "On behalf of the Billings alumni committee, I'd like to congratulate you on your presidency."

"Thank you," I said, surprised that news of my presidency had made it to the board of directors. Her formality made me feel flustered and warm—unsure of how to respond—and the box felt big and awkward in my arms. Sabine shifted in her seat and I cleared my throat, tipping my head toward her side of the room as I eyed Noelle pointedly.

"Oh, and this is Sabine DuLac," Noelle added flatly.

My face burned for Sabine. Why was Noelle so very disinterested in my roommate? But Sabine didn't seem to notice the tone. She was focused intently on Suzel. At the beginning of the semester, when Cheyenne had made all of the Billings newbies steal artifacts from around Easton, Sabine had chosen to lift Susan Llewelyn's valedictorian banner from the chapel. Sabine had spent hours researching Suzel in the Easton library and was fascinated by her.

"It's an honor to meet you," Sabine said, getting up to shake Suzel's hand.

My heart fluttered with nerves. Oh, crap. Should I have shaken her hand? But she had put this huge box right into my arms. Suddenly I wished I had paid attention when Sabine had told me all those little factoids she'd learned about Suzel, just so that I could have an interesting or insightful question to ask. I quickly turned around and placed the box on my desk, knocking over my cup of pens and pencils in the process. I was so mortified I wanted to cry. Noelle pressed her lips together at the huge clatter, but Suzel ignored it.

"And you," Suzel said politely to Sabine. "One of our newest initiates."

Sabine and I glanced at each other. She had, in fact, never been properly initiated. But neither of us was about to mention that debacle. On the night of the annual ritual, Cheyenne had made sure that the girls she had deemed acceptable—Missy, Kiki, and Astrid—had been welcomed to our circle with open arms, while Sabine, Constance, and Lorna had been humiliated and ostracized. The whole thing had been busted up by Headmaster Cromwell; Cheyenne had been expelled and had taken her life that night. No one had spoken about initiation since.

"Well, that is for you, obviously," Suzel said, looking at the gift as she folded her hands in front of her. "Open it later, when you are alone," she added firmly.

I glanced at Sabine, who seemed discomfited by the instruction. "Oh. Okay. Thank you," I stammered.

"We all think you're going to be a real asset to the Billings legacy, Reed," Suzel said, her smile broadening as she looked me up and down. Thank goodness I had worn the new, expensive sweater Noelle had given me.

"Thank you. I hope I live up to your expectations," I said. There. At least that was a full sentence.

"It was so nice to meet you both," Suzel said.

"You too," I said. "Will we see you at the alumni dinner on Saturday?"

Yes! Another complete sentence. Suzel smiled.

"Absolutely. I wouldn't miss it," she replied. "I'll see you then."

Then she shook both our hands and walked toward the door. Noelle showed her out and, after a few hushed words in the hallway, came back inside.

"So that was Suzel, huh?" I asked. Aside from Sabine stealing Suzel's chapel banner, I hadn't heard Susan Llewelyn's name since last year, when she had wrangled a way for all of us to get off campus for a spa day. Us being myself, Noelle, Ariana, Kiran, Taylor, and Natasha. It seemed a million years ago.

"That was Suzel," Noelle said with a smile.

"Well? Come on, Reed. Open your gift!" Sabine urged me, eyeing the package hungrily.

"Oh, yeah!" I said. I turned to pick up the box.

"Reed, no," Noelle said, placing her hand on top of the package.

"What? Why not?" I asked.

"You heard Suzel. You're supposed to open it when you're alone," she said, pointedly looking at Sabine.

Sabine turned positively ashen. And why not? It seemed obvious that Noelle knew what was in the box. And soon I would know what was in the box. Noelle was basically saying Sabine was the only one in the room unworthy of knowing.

"Well, yeah, but—"

"Reed, you're president of Billings House. You have to take these things seriously," Noelle said sternly.

I swallowed hard and looked at Sabine. Since the beginning of the year, she had become one of my best friends, and I felt awful leaving her out. But what was I going to do? This was official Billings business. This was big. "She's right. I'm sorry."

Sabine shrugged. "Fine. Whatever." Then she turned and went back to her desk as if she couldn't have cared less.

But I knew that she did. It was obvious that she did. When it came to Billings stuff, Sabine just didn't understand. I hoped that as time went on she would figure out how lucky she was to be here, and what it really meant. Otherwise, I had a feeling this presidency thing was going to become a real issue between us.

ABSOLUTE POWER

It was a Chloé bag. A big, black, buttery, limited-edition leather Chloé bag. Worth at least two thousand dollars, which I only knew because Portia had a similar one and I'd overheard her telling Shelby about how she had been on the list to get one for over a year, and how her dad had freaked when he saw the bill. Even though he was supposedly some big, international billionaire. He dabbled in something to do with gold and diamonds—and had shady dealings with underground militia in several different countries, if you believed the whispers.

"One bag? One bag?" Mr. Ahronian kept saying over and over again in his thick Armenian accent, turning redder and redder with each parroted phrase—which Portia and her mother had found hilarious, apparently.

But he had, of course, paid for it in the end.

And now I had one. Me. Reed Brennan. If I sold this thing on eBay I could pay off my dad's car loan. Not that I was about to do that. This thing was just way too yummy. I was allowed to have something yummy, wasn't I?

I glanced over my shoulder to double-check that I was alone. Then I lifted the bag to my face with both hands and inhaled. That tartly rich smell of new leather filled my senses and made my head feel light. I think I was in love.

But why couldn't I open this in front of Sabine? It was outrageous, sure, but she was going to see me carrying it eventually. Me. Scholarship student Reed Brennan with a two-thousand-dollar bag. Sure I had received some expensive gifts from Kiran and the others last year, but nothing like this.

I ran my fingertips over the soft leather, toyed with the gold closure, and was about to set it down so I could lean back and just admire it, when I realized there was something inside. I opened the top flap and peeked in. Placed neatly in the bag were a thick, glossy Neiman Marcus catalog, a jewel case with a CD inside, and a long, red clutch with a zipper. Which was bulging. Something in there as well.

This was like Christmas morning. Only no Christmas morning I'd ever had. I pulled out the clutch and popped it open. Fendi. But this time it wasn't the label that stopped me. It was the wad of cash nestled inside the clutch.

No. Freaking. Way.

I snapped it shut and glanced over my shoulder again. Dead silence. Everyone was downstairs talking about our masquerade ball.

I planned on joining them in a few minutes, but I was going to have to get over this heart attack I was having first.

Hands shaking, I opened the clutch again and pulled out the paper-banded stack of money. I'd never seen so many hundreds before. The printing on the white band read $5,000.

Five thousand dollars. Cash. Why would anyone want to give me five thousand dollars cash?

Gulping in air, I shoved the money back in the clutch and shoved the clutch under my pillow, feeling like a SWAT team was going to burst in at any moment and throw me up against the wall. Five thousand dollars. That was more money than I'd ever dreamed of having in my hands. What was it for?

I took a deep breath and went back over to the bag. I placed the CD next to my closed laptop. Then I pulled out the catalog. There was a note attached.

> Dear Reed,
>
> Congratulations on being elected president of Billings. As vice president of purchasing for Neiman Marcus Group, I am pleased to find myself in a position to offer you an open line of credit. I'll be sending you our look book each season, from which you may select up to a thousand dollars' worth of merchandise, gratis. Enjoy!
>
> Yours in Billings,
> Tinsley Dunellen
> Easton Academy Class of 1990

This was too much. Free money. Free clothes. Free designer bags. What next? A free trip to Hawaii?

Beyond intrigued, I opened my computer and popped the CD in. I had to clutch my sides to keep from trembling with excitement as it whirred to life. Then a list of folders popped up in the center of the screen.

BILLINGS ALUMNI 1980s
BILLINGS ALUMNI 1990s
CURRENT BILLINGS RESIDENTS
BILLINGS ALUMNI FUND
REAL ESTATE HOLDINGS
UNIVERSITY CONTACTS
FORTUNE 500 CONTACTS
LOS ANGELES
NEW YORK
PARIS
MILAN

And on and on. I opened file after file. The alumni fund balance was in the millions, and I now knew the pin number. There were contacts in the admissions departments at every prestigious university in the country and at dozens of elite international corporations where anyone would want to work. The city files had contact info organized by city and then by company. The real estate holdings folder contained one huge document listing homes owned by Billings alums all over the world, which were, apparently, at our disposal should we need to, oh, jet off to Dubai at a moment's notice or hole up on the shores of the Mediterranean for a few days. There was contact information for every Billings alum, plus personal info on whom they had married when, how many children they had, how many homes they owned and where. Plus, each entry had a file marked "pertinent info," which turned out to be "pertinent dirt." Dirt on each of our esteemed alumni. Affairs and arrests and compromising situations. As I read, I started to blush. Why would this be here? Why would anyone want to give this to me? Who had compiled this stuff and how did they know about all these indiscretions?

And did the file on the current residents have the same kind of info?

I hated myself, but I had to know. I went to the current resident file and sure enough, inside were seventeen files, each named for one of my fellow Billings Girls. Including Noelle and Cheyenne. Ignoring my morbid curiosity about Cheyenne, I opened my own file. And there it all was. My family's income. My father's job. My mother's entire, mortifying medical history. My brother's GPA at Penn State. And tons of info on me. Records I'd broken at Croton High. The fact that I'd won firsts the last two quarters of sophomore year. The job I'd held over the summer and exactly how much money I had made.

It was positively disturbing seeing all these personal facts of my own life laid out before me like they were nothing. Those paranoid feelings I sometimes had that I was being watched? Turned out they weren't so paranoid after all.

At least whoever was watching me didn't seem to know about that almost kiss with Dash over the summer. Listed under significant relationships were only Adam Robinson, my one Croton boyfriend; Thomas Pearson (deceased); Walter Whittaker (attended Legacy with); and Joshua Hollis (current).

I sat back in my chair for a moment, considering the folders of my fellow Billings Girls. Missy Thurber. Wouldn't mind having some dirt on her. Portia Ahronian. What, exactly, did her mysterious father do for a living, anyway? And Cheyenne Martin. Did she have a history of depression? Erratic behavior? Seeing something like that in her folder would have made me feel so much better.

But could I do it? Could I really read about the innermost secrets of these people who were supposed to be my friends? It was such a violation.

Although . . . Cheyenne was dead. And if there was something in there that might make me feel less guilty, less anxious . . .

My fingers hovered over the mouse. I was just about to click when my new iPhone sang at me so loudly I almost fell out of my chair.

I grabbed it up in both hands. Josh's face appeared on the screen. I could barely hold the phone as I brought it to my ear.

"Hello?"

"Reed? Are you okay?" he asked.

I suppose I did sound a tad stressed.

"Yeah. Fine. Sorry," I said. I quickly closed all the files and ejected the CD. "Just startled by the phone."

"Sorry. Listen, I'm outside. Can you come down?" he said.

"You're outside? Now?" I asked, getting up. My knees were like pudding from everything I'd seen, everything I'd learned, all the possibilities. I shoved the curtain aside, and there Josh was, on the grass below my window. He lifted his free hand and smiled sheepishly.

"I'll be right there."

I turned off the phone, shut down my computer, and stashed the CD in the back of my CD case, behind an old John Mayer CD. No one—not even the mysterious Billings P.I. Squad—would be looking there. The catalog I shoved back in the Chloé bag; then I placed the whole thing under my desk and put the chair in front of it as camouflage.

Right now, all this was mine and mine alone. And I wanted to savor it.

NAUGHTY

Josh shifted from foot to foot as I walked over to him, tugging down the sleeves of my sweater. It was a cool night, and he was wearing a high-necked, zip-front, ribbed sweater that was basically the sexiest thing he owned. Even though we hadn't talked since our minor blow-out that morning, it made me want to sink into his arms and kiss him. Or maybe I was just high from my power trip.

"So, basically, I'm a jerk," he said by way of greeting.

I took his arm and pulled him closer to the side of the building. Technically, we weren't supposed to be out of our dorms this late, let alone participating in a mixed-sex rendezvous. Not that the rules had ever stopped anyone before. Still, I couldn't help thinking of the "pertinent info" file and wondering if this would somehow end up in it.

"You're not a jerk," I whispered.

"Yeah. I am." He scratched the back of his head and looked at his feet. "Look, Noelle is never going to be my favorite person, but she's important to you, and I should have realized that. I'll . . . I'll try to get along with her from now on."

I gazed at Josh, beyond touched. "You don't have to do that. I mean, I understand why you don't like her. I really do. Maybe we can just, I don't know, hang out separately or something."

"Yeah. Like that's possible," Josh joked. I loved his smile. His sweet, self-effacing smile. "No. It's okay. I can keep my mouth shut. Really. I'll be good."

"Well, maybe you can just do other things with your mouth," I said, stepping closer to him.

Josh's eyes lit up. "Really? What did you have in mind?"

I snaked my arms around his neck and pulled him to me. As always, the moment his tongue touched mine I felt a pleasant shiver all the way down to my toes and an involuntary moan escaped my throat. Josh took this as a signal and deepened the kiss, backing me toward the outer wall of Billings. Something about the open air, the conspicuousness of it all, made me completely and totally hot. I pulled him closer to me, pressing his whole body into mine, and his hands slid under my sweater.

I couldn't believe we were doing this. Right there in the middle of campus when any one of the many security guards could have strolled right by. But I was president of Billings now. Didn't that mean I was untouchable? It didn't matter anyway. I couldn't have stopped for anything. Make-up groping was sexy enough as it was, but make-up groping with the possibility of getting caught was downright naughty.

Josh's fingers found my bra and he cupped one of my breasts

gently. I couldn't breathe. The second his fingertips found their way under the cotton, however, I broke away.

Okay. Not here. Not now.

"What?" he said blearily. "Sorry. I—"

"No. It's okay," I said quickly. "I just . . . we're so gonna get caught."

"God. You're right. I—"

His eyes flicked up to my right and his skin paled.

"What?" I said, petrified now. I stumbled away from the wall and looked up at the window, but there was nothing there. "Was someone watching us?"

"No. I don't think so," Josh said quickly. "I guess I'm just paranoid."

"You should go," I said quickly. I gave him a quick kiss on the mouth as I pushed him back.

"Okay. Yeah." Reluctantly, he turned to leave, then snapped his fingers and faced me again. "I almost forgot. . . . I wanted to ask you. . . . The big Hollis family reunion is being held in Maine next weekend. Wanna come?"

"The Hollis family reunion?" I asked.

"Yeah. Every year my dad gets the whole clan together at our house in Maine for this massive clambake," Josh said, tucking his hands under his arms. "Cousins and aunts and great-aunts and everything fly in from all over the country. And they *all* want to meet you."

I almost choked on my own saliva. "They all want to meet *me*?"

"Well, they don't all know who you are . . . yet. But once they do, they'll want to meet you," Josh replied. "My mom personally asked me to invite you, and my brothers and sisters are basically dying to see who this hottie is that I couldn't stop talking about all summer. It's really just Saturday, then we'd stay overnight and come right back on Sunday. So are you in?"

I hesitated. Clearly this meant a lot to Josh, but a huge group of new people I was supposed to impress? That didn't sound like a fun way to spend a weekend.

"Come on. It'll be great," Josh said, stepping closer and reaching for my hand. "I promise I won't leave your side the entire time."

I grinned. "Well, when you put it that way . . ."

"Yes! I'm so going to win the Hottest New Girlfriend trophy this year," Josh said, making a fist with his free hand. "Suck it, Hunter Hollis! Your reign ends now."

"What?"

"Kidding! I'm just kidding!" He gave me a peck on the lips. "I love you."

"I love you too," I replied with a happy smile.

He waved before jogging off, and as I watched him go, something moved in the corner of my vision. My heart stopped and I looked up again. The curtain in one of the hallway windows dropped down, as if someone had just been holding it back.

You're just imagining things, Reed. No one's watching you.

A sudden chill raced down my back and I glanced over my shoulder. Nothing but twinkling lights along the stone walks, and trees swaying in the breeze. But I was still freaked. I tugged my sweater closer to my body and ran the last few steps, ducking through the door. Once inside, I felt foolish and shook my head. I decided not to think about phantom spies and instead focus on the new issue at hand: an entire weekend feeling like a totally awkward outsider amongst one of America's oldest, most elite families. Taking a deep breath, I mounted the steps to my room and resigned myself to my fate. It was just one day. I could get through it.

For Josh.

EVERY HOUR

Friday night, the alumni descended on the Easton campus like locusts. They were everywhere. Taking group photos in front of dorms, chatting in the center of the cafeteria, checking out our newly opened Coffee Carma. Any student whose parents or siblings were not among the visiting, or those who just didn't feel like kissing ass, hid out in their dorms. I was one of the hermits. I knew that as the new president of Billings I should have been out there networking, but I couldn't bring myself to leave my room. Not when there was the possibility of bumping into Dash.

He had never told me whether he planned to attend. And after a blissful week with Josh, talking, holding hands, and sneaking in more hot-and-heavy make-out sessions wherever and whenever we could, I was more resolved than ever to cut Dash out of my life. The fact that Noelle and I were hanging out every day helped make the decision even easier. I'd read the few e-mails Dash had sent me that week, but

I hadn't replied. There hadn't been any more mushy stuff, thank God, and I liked to think I had imagined the whole thing. It made it that much easier to put it behind me.

But there was something else. Something that had proven much more difficult to leave in the past. All week I had tried not to think about Cheyenne's e-mail. Had tried to put it out of my mind. I had even set her e-mail address as spam so that if the e-mail *had* been set to repeat send, it would go directly into my computer's recycle bin. Every time I thought about it, I told myself that it was over. That as long as I didn't check that recycle bin, I'd never have to see that e-mail again.

But now it was Friday night and I had to know. Had to know if I had imagined the whole thing. Or if it had been some random glitch. Or if Cheyenne had really been evil enough to make sure I received her message of blame from beyond the grave every week. Nervous with dread, I sat up late in bed, pretending to study under the warm glow of my book light. I said good night to Sabine and she, as always, passed out quickly. As soon as I heard her breathing regulate, my heart skipped a beat. The moment had arrived

I shoved my covers aside and quietly placed my history book on the floor. My computer was on sleep mode, so it popped right to life when I opened it. My fingers trembled as I reached for the mouse, and I told myself to chill. There wouldn't be anything there. It had been a glitch. That was the most obvious explanation.

First, I checked my inbox. Nothing. My heartbeat slowed slightly. I glanced at the recycle bin.

I had to check it. Of course I did. If I didn't check it, I would never really know who Cheyenne had been. What she had intended for me. Whether she had really, truly, meant what she had written. Meant it so much she never wanted me to forget it.

I held my breath and clicked open the recycle bin. The gasp that escaped me was loud enough to wake the dead. Even to wake Sabine.

"Reed?" she asked blearily, sitting up. She pushed her thick black hair out of her face. "What is it?"

I couldn't answer. Couldn't tear my eyes from the list of previously unseen e-mails.

SENDER: Cheyenne Martin
SENDER: Cheyenne Martin
SENDER: Cheyenne Martin
SENDER: Cheyenne Martin
SENDER: Cheyenne Martin
SENDER: Cheyenne Martin

It went on forever. For pages. I clicked and scrolled, clicked and scrolled. For three days the e-mail had been coming to me every hour. Every. Hour. And three days was all my recycle bin could hold. It would automatically delete anything beyond that. Had the e-mail actually been coming all week long?

"Reed? You're scaring me. What's wrong?"

Sabine was getting up now. Crossing the room. Panicked, I somehow found the "delete all" button with my mouse and clicked. The file was empty when she arrived.

"Are you all right?" Sabine asked me.

She laid her hand on my shoulder, and I jumped up as if scorched. Startled, Sabine took a step back.

"Sorry. I'm sorry. I just . . . don't feel very well," I managed to say.

Then I tore by her for the bathroom, slamming the door behind me. Gripping the sides of the cold white sink with both hands, I heaved for breath. This wasn't happening. It couldn't be happening.

"Reed?" Sabine asked from the other side of the door.

I flipped on the cold water full blast. "I'll be right out!"

After several splashes to the face, I was feeling calmer. More rational. Obviously, it was a computer glitch. Obviously. But if it was, why would it start out sending the e-mail once a week and then randomly switch to once every hour?

"It doesn't matter how it happened—it just did," I muttered to my reflection. "Now all you have to do is figure out a way to work the problem."

Thinking proactively calmed my pulse to an almost normal rate. I was in control. I could fix this. I turned off the water and stared at the mirror. Stared into my own eyes. Tomorrow I would change my e-mail address. That would put an end to this insanity. Once and for all.

DASH

Saturday night, thanks to the Driscoll Alumni Dinner, I was finally forced to come out of hiding, and after the night before, I was more than ready to get away from my computer and my room. With a new e-mail address and a new password all set up, I was confident that I had heard from Cheyenne Martin for the last time. It was time to rejoin the land of the living.

The Driscoll Dinner was being held at the same posh hotel my friends and I had lunched at the week before. It was Headmaster Cromwell's pet project. At the beginning of the year, when he'd made all the students sign up for a committee, Sabine and I had joined the waitstaff. So I was to spend Saturday night dressed in a black skirt and white tuxedo top, serving hors d'oeuvres to illustrious alums.

And if Dash happened to be there, there was no hope of avoiding him.

As I circulated the loud, packed Driscoll ballroom with my tray of crab puffs, carefully avoiding silk gowns and wingtip shoes, my heart pitter-pattered uncomfortably. Maybe he'd decided not to come. This was kind of a stodgy event, after all. Surely a Yale freshman had better things to do with his time than schmooze with the elderly set. A kegger or a poetry reading or something must have been calling his name.

A half hour of grinning and serving and small-talking went by without a glimpse of him, and I finally started to relax. Cocktail hour would be over in thirty minutes. All I had to do was get through this and then I could spend the rest of the night hiding out in the kitchen, maybe even sneak in some pantry smooching with Josh. I was practically home free.

And then, as I turned away from a group of pin-striped Wall Street types with booming voices, a hand gripped my upper arm. I almost dropped my tray, but saved it two inches before it could make the clatter heard round the world.

It was him. It was him.

"Hey. You look sexy in that uniform."

My lungs filled with air. It wasn't him. It was Josh.

"Thanks," I said, hoping he'd attribute my blush to his flattery.

He looked adorable in his black tux, a long white tie tucked into his jacket. His curls were, as always, doing their own thing, but their disheveled state only made the whole look all the more perfect. What could be hotter than a scruffy artist all suited up? Josh slid his eyes from side to side and, finding the coast generally clear, leaned in to kiss me.

Ah, Josh. Josh. Josh. Josh. Josh.

He smiled teasingly when he pulled away. "I'll be checking on things in the kitchen if you want to pick up where that left off."

See? We even think the same. We're so perfect for each other.

"Noted," I said with a grin.

He turned around jauntily. I took a deep breath to calm my skipping heart and turned the other way.

Where I found myself face to face with Dash.

Okay. He was even more gorgeous than I remembered. Broader. Taller. More chiseled. Completely at home in his perfect tux. His usually warm brown eyes were piercing. His blond hair fell casually over his forehead as he looked me dead in the eye. *Smoldering* was the only word that came to mind.

"Dash," I heard myself say—gasp, really. This guy had almost kissed me last summer. This Adonis of perfection had almost kissed *me*.

Dash stared at me for a long moment. Then he glanced past me at, I could only assume, my retreating boyfriend—his friend. His jaw worked, as if he was trying to hold something back.

What? *What*?

"We need to talk," he said to me.

And he didn't even bother to check whether the coast was clear. He simply took my free hand and led me away.

JUST FRIENDS

It took Dash five seconds to find a secluded hallway near the back of the hotel. Clearly he had been here before. I dropped my half-empty tray on a random chair and wiped my palms on my skirt. I was so panicked I thought I might vomit. Or wet myself. Or both. What if Josh had seen us leave the room? What if Noelle had? What if Missy had seen us and told everyone? Which was so something she'd do.

I instantly thought of that as-yet-unopened folder on the Billings CD. If Missy decided to wage war, I'd have the ammo to fight back. But why was I thinking about this now? Now, when my fingers were completely enveloped in Dash's warm, strong hand? When Josh was waiting for me in the kitchen.

He ducked into an alcove, then looked out and double-checked the hallway.

"We're alone," he said fervently.

I just looked at him. I didn't know what to say. Why had he brought me here? Why the intensity?

He's just going to tell me he's back together with Noelle. That they were, I don't know, apart for a while and now they're back together. Or he's going to warn me, now that she's back, to not tell her we've been corresponding. As if I needed that particular caveat.

"You didn't e-mail me back this week," he said. His eyes were sad. Dare I say desperate?

I pressed my hands into the cool wall behind me, grounding myself. "I—"

"I was worried something happened to you," he said, taking a step closer to me. "Are you okay?"

I had no idea what to make of this. "I'm fine," I said, acutely aware that mere inches separated us.

He seemed confused for a moment, but then his face cleared and he blew out a breath.

"Good. Okay. Good," he said, cupping the back of his neck with his hand. He turned away from me and tipped his head back as if he was struggling with something, working his neck muscles with his fingers. When he looked at me again, his eyes searched mine. "Reed, there's something you need to know."

Suddenly, I felt so disloyal I wanted to die. Just the sound of his deep, confident voice saying my name sent shivers through me. All I wanted was to hear him say my name again and again. How could I feel this way? I loved Josh. I knew I loved Josh. But standing this close to Dash . . .

"I know we never say anything like this to each other. I've avoided it up until now. But you should know that Noelle and I are not together."

I took a step back. Now all of me pressed into the wall. It was the only way to keep myself upright. He actually liked me. Why else would he tell me this? Why else would he be looking at me with such obvious longing in his eyes?

"Does that have any effect on you whatsoever?" he asked.

This was it. The moment of truth. What I said right now could define me forever. I was either going to be a loyal, trustworthy girlfriend, or an unfaithful fiend.

"No," I said, lifting my chin. My voice cracked, dammit. I cleared it and tried again. "Why should it?"

Dash was clearly stunned. Hurt. He drew himself up and looked at me incredulously. "Oh. Okay. My mistake," he said. He turned, but then looked back at me again as if I were an apparition. "I just thought . . . No. Forget it."

He turned to go. Something inside of me snapped and I shoved myself away from the wall. I couldn't let him leave. Not yet. Not like this. I hated that I had hurt him.

"Dash, wait," I blurted.

He stopped but didn't turn around. I could hear him breathing.

"We're still friends, right?" I said. Pathetic, I know. But what else could I say?

"Friends."

He laughed derisively. Then he turned around and backed me

right into the wall again. So fast I barely even saw it coming. My heart pounded in my throat as he braced his hands above my head and leaned in toward me. My chest heaved up a down, up and down. My brain went hazy. His lips were inches from mine. Millimeters. I stared into his eyes, lost. No control. No control. No control.

He loomed even closer. Every last inch of me throbbed. I could practically taste his breath. Dash McCafferty was going to kiss me. Dash McCafferty was going to kiss me. And I was going to let him.

He smiled. My heart stopped.

"Sure," he whispered, sending chills all through my body. "All we are is friends."

He backed up a step, and oxygen whooshed in at me from all angles.

"I'll keep telling myself that, if that's what you want me to do," he said solemnly.

He backed all the way out of the alcove, never taking his eyes off mine, and was gone.

PERFECTLY GOOD
EXPLANATIONS

Sunday night, Sabine was in the shower in our adjoining bathroom and I finally felt free to open an e-mail that had been sitting in my inbox all day. An e-mail from Dash. I don't know whether it was the fact that I had seen it there that morning, or whether it was the things he had said to me at the Driscoll, but I hadn't been able to stop thinking about him all day. Knowing that a guy like Dash could like a girl like me was intoxicating. I'll admit it. And as much as I tried to lock him out of my thoughts and conjure up Josh, Dash kept pounding his way back in. It was amazing how thinking about someone could make me feel like the scum of the earth, but totally exhilarated at the same time. What the e-mail could possibly contain, I had no idea, but I was so nervous as I attempted to open it that my fingers slipped off the mouse from all the sweat. I took a deep breath, wiped my hands on my jeans, and opened the e-mail.

Reed,

It was good to see you last night. Hope the rest of your
weekend goes well.

Dash

Okay. What the hell did that mean? Had I really waited all day to
be alone to read that crap? Maybe it was some sort of dig at my "just
friends" thing. Maybe he was showing me how very well he could play
along. Was he mocking me?

I was just reading it over again, as if there could be any hidden
meaning in so few words, when the door to my room opened behind
me. I slapped the laptop closed without even thinking about it. Thank
God I did. Noelle was on top of me in less than two seconds.

"Secret pen pal?" she asked wryly, eyeing the computer.

I retasted the turkey club I'd had for lunch right about then.

"What? No. Why? I—"

The door opened again and this time it was Portia. She was sucking on a huge iced coffee and looked wired enough to power the whole
dorm.

"Check your e-mail! I just forwarded you something!"

The last thing I wanted to do was open my computer. But Noelle was
temporarily distracted by Portia's manic state, so I quickly popped it
open and deleted Dash's message. Way too close for my comfort. At
the top of my inbox was a forwarded message from Portia titled "FW:
LEGACY LIVES!"

"What's this?"

"Open the attachment!" Portia demanded, taking a drag on her oversize purple straw. Her pupils were like pinpoints.

I clicked the attachment. An Adobe file opened on my screen. A scanned-in image of what looked like a very expensive, hand-lettered invitation. An invitation to the Legacy. October 31st. Location TBD. Entry tokens to follow.

"One of my friends at Dalton sent it to me. They all got them in the mail yesterday," Portia informed us, wide-eyed. "Is it some kind of hoax, or is it not canceled? And how come we didn't get any?"

"I told you guys someone would throw it," Noelle said, casually checking her hair in the mirror above my dresser. She lifted it back from her face and sucked in her already perfect cheeks, checking herself out from side to side. "I'm sure our invites will come tomorrow."

"You think? Oh my God. Thank God!" Portia trilled. "Senior year without the Legacy would have sucked."

I smiled for them, but inside I couldn't help feeling stepped on. So much for the Billings Masquerade idea. Everyone was obviously going to want to go to the Legacy. Where I couldn't, in fact, go at all. What kind of Billings president couldn't even get into the biggest party of the year? The lame kind, I supposed.

"Hey! That's a nice shot of you and Cheyenne!" Portia practically shouted.

My heart constricted. I turned around to follow her gaze and had to close my computer lid to see what she was pointing at. There, pinned to the mostly bare bulletin board behind my desk, was the picture of me and Cheyenne from Vienna's Sweet Seventeen. The very picture that was supposed to be hidden in the bottom of my bottom desk drawer in the back of a sophomore English book.

"Omigod," I said, pushing back from my desk and standing up. "How the hell did that get there?"

Not a soul had been around when I'd hidden it over a week ago. How had it ended up on my bulletin board?

"Reed, chill," Noelle said. "What's the problem?"

"I didn't put that there," I told her, shaking. "I stashed it in the bottom of my desk. I don't understand—"

Sabine walked out of the bathroom, removing a thick white towel from her hair. She took one look at me and her face creased with concern. "Reed? What's wrong?"

"That picture. Do you know how it got there?" I asked her.

Sabine squinted at my desk. "It's been there, no?"

I looked at the photo wildly. Had it been? Had I pinned it there and simply forgotten? Was I totally losing my mind?

"No!" I said, shaking my head adamantly. "I hid it. I—"

"Reed, stop," Noelle demanded. "This is not a big deal. The cleaning service was here this morning. They probably found it and thought you lost it or something. They probably thought they were being helpful."

"You think?" I asked, my hand over my heart.

"I know. My stuff is always moved around after they've been here. Just be grateful they didn't steal anything." Noelle reached over and yanked out the pin, removing the photo, which she quickly shoved right back into the bottom drawer. "See? All better."

As soon as the photo was gone, my heart rate started to return to normal again. Noelle was right. It was a perfectly good explanation. I wasn't insane. I wasn't.

There were perfectly good explanations for all the strange things that had been happening to me lately.

I was just glad there were people around to tell me what those explanations were.

SNUBBED

On Monday afternoon between classes, the solarium was buzzing with the news about the Legacy. Half the student body had jammed the campus post office after lunch, and nothing. The mail had been delivered, but there wasn't a single Legacy invite among all the catalogs and college applications and postcards from exotic locales. Everyone knew someone from another school who had received one. It seemed clear that Easton's legacies were, for some reason, being snubbed. And these people were not accustomed to being snubbed. As I wove through the crowded, sun-streaked room, packed with people sipping their mochaccinos and foaming lattes, I caught snippets of indignant conversations.

"Barton got them on Friday. Friday! And that's right up the road—"

"Dalton shouldn't even be invited. I mean, day schools? Please. Next they're gonna extend it to those crunchy satellite places with, like, no grades."

"If we don't get invited, I'm gonna sue. I swear."

I joined the back of the line at the Coffee Carma counter and Noelle slipped in behind me. "We're about to have a Million Moron March on our hands."

I laughed and glanced around. "The coffee can't be helping. I think you can get a buzz just by breathing the air in here."

"Please. This student body has built up enough tolerance to put all the rejects at Promises, Wonderland, and Betty Ford to shame," Noelle joked. "A little caffeine is not going to affect them."

As Noelle looked over her shoulder, her expression darkened. My classmate Diana Waters and a group of girls from Pemberly stood a few feet away, whispering and staring at Noelle.

"Problem?" Noelle asked.

Diana blanched. "Um, no. No problem. We were just . . ." She looked down quickly. "Nice boots."

"They're Balenciaga," Noelle replied, giving them a cursory look. "And if you don't walk away right now, you'll find out what they look like up your ass."

Because I liked Diana, I hid my laugh behind my hand as she and her friends quickly found a table at the back of the room.

"That keeps happening," Noelle said, looking bored as she surveyed the menu behind the counter. "Like no one's ever threatened their way back in here before."

We both knew that wasn't why they were staring. They were staring because of what she and the others had done to Thomas. If Noelle had been intimidating last year, her presence was now morbidly fascinating, even scary. She was practically a walking urban legend.

Noelle and I ordered our coffees, and I paid for both with my Carma Card. When we turned around, Gage was bearing down on us.

"Okay. What the hell is going on?" he demanded. His hair was flattened, highlighted with blond streaks, and cut short. He had day-old stubble all over his chin. Plus he was wearing an L.A. Galaxy soccer jersey, even though he didn't play soccer.

"The Beckham makeover, huh? How original," Noelle commented.

"Right. Because you're so above trends," Gage replied with a sneer. "For your information, while I was in the city this weekend I saw ten of these bogus Legacy invitations with my own eyes. These things are for real and we don't have any."

Josh stepped up behind Gage and leaned over to give me a kiss. "If they're bogus, how can they also be real?" Josh questioned, raising an eyebrow.

"Shut up, man. I'm not in the mood," Gage snapped.

"Sorry," Josh said, trying not to laugh. Which made me laugh.

"Oh, I'm really glad this is so funny to you," Gage said derisively. "But if Easton has been blackballed by the Legacy, we're over. We're gonna be shut out of everything. We may as well just go enroll at some public school and call it a day. We have to find out what the hell is going on."

Both Gage and Noelle looked at me expectantly. I realized with a start that they were waiting for me to say something. That they were expecting *me* to find out what the hell was going on. Noelle Lange and Gage Coolidge. Looking to me.

And then I remembered. I was president of Billings. In theory, the most connected girl at Easton. I thought of all the info I had back in my room. All those powerful people I could contact. Somewhere in there, there had to be an answer.

"Don't worry," I told them, feeling a sudden surge of adrenaline. "Whatever it is, I'll figure it out."

Noelle nodded approvingly and Gage seemed pacified by my promise. Josh reached out and laced his fingers though mine. A flutter of pride welled up inside me. Once again I felt very Noelle Lange, but this time Noelle Lange was standing right there.

Very weird. But also very, very cool.

REVOLUTIONARY

I had Dash's cell phone number from over the summer at the Vineyard. He'd given it to both me and Natasha so we could make plans to go sailing. I'd never used it. Instead, Natasha had called him and set it all up. We'd gone out on her dad's boat one afternoon, and Dash had brought two of his ridiculously gorgeous male cousins and a case of beer along. All very innocent. Until the following night at the restaurant where I'd worked, when we'd shared that almost kiss . . .

Anyway, I had never used it. Until now.

I needed more information. That was my excuse. And aside from Natasha—who I knew had a Monday night class at Dartmouth—Dash was the only Easton alumni I was still in contact with. Well, and Whittaker. I supposed I could have gotten Constance to call Whittaker.

But whatever. It was just a quick question and good-bye. I hit the send button and crossed my legs on my bed, holding my breath as it rang. He answered right away.

"Hi."

His tone was intimate. Relieved. Maybe he didn't know it was me.

"Hey. It's me, Reed," I said.

He chuckled. "I know. There's this amazing new thing called caller ID."

I laughed, relaxing slightly. After his cold e-mail, this was a promising reception.

"This is a pleasant surprise. How are you?" he asked. Again husky. Intimate. I was blushing. I glanced at my desk. At the framed picture of me and Josh, and cleared my throat.

"I'm fine. Actually, I was calling because I have a question," I told him, all business.

"I'm listening," he replied. I heard female voices in the background and someone giggled. Suddenly my eyes burned. "Hang on. Let me go out in the hall," he said.

As I waited I realized my fists were clenched and I relaxed my fingers. I was not jealous. I could not be jealous.

"Sorry about that," he said. "I'm alone now."

"Having a party?" I asked.

"Something like that. Our sailing team won the Hood Trophy yesterday and we're still kind of celebrating. It's kind of a big deal around here," he said lightly.

"Oh. That's great. Congrats," I said, even though I had no idea what a Hood Trophy was. But if they were celebrating, then where were all the guys from his team? Unless they had very effeminate voices, they weren't present. "I heard you were the only freshman on the team,"

I said, ignoring the jealous questions that were itching my tongue. "That's incredible."

"Thanks. So what's up?" he asked.

I was dying to know why he hadn't told me about the team—whether he was just being modest or whether I wasn't important enough to share such things with, but I couldn't do that without sounding like a petulant loser. A petulant loser who was *not* okay with being just friends.

"Reed?"

Right. Focus, Reed. He's not your boyfriend, and you have a job to do. I took a deep breath.

"It's about the Legacy. Have you heard what's going on?" I asked.

"Something about it being canceled, then not being canceled. . . ."

"Yeah, well, now every school on the East Coast has gotten invites except for Easton," I told him. I gave myself major props for staying on point.

"That's odd," Dash said.

"So, I know you wouldn't be getting one anyway—"

"Ouch." He laughed.

"But have any of your alumni friends gotten them?" I asked.

"Now that you mention it, no one's brought it up," Dash replied. "Usually the guys plan a whole weekend around the thing—even for us unsavories who don't merit an actual invite to the party—and I haven't heard a thing. Not even from Whit, who as you know, lives for this stuff."

Just then the door opened and my heart hit my throat. It was only

Sabine, who smiled at me as she crossed the room, but I still felt as if I'd just been snagged.

"Do you want me to make some calls? Find out for sure?" Dash was saying.

"No, actually. That's okay. I have a plan," I lied, wanting to get off the phone as soon as possible now that I had an audience.

"Reed, listen, about Saturday—"

"Actually, I can't talk about it right now," I said quickly, as Sabine shot me a quizzical glance. "I'll talk to you later. And thanks."

"Wait! I—"

I ended the call and turned the phone off for good measure, tossing it on my bed as I stood.

"What's up?" I asked Sabine, shoving my hands into the back pockets of my jeans. "How was your lab?"

"Fine. It was a lab," she said with a laugh. "Why so red? Were you talking with Josh?" she said teasingly.

The lump of guilt in my throat was barely swallowable. "No. Just . . . my brother," I said dismissively.

It was beyond obvious that she didn't believe me, but she simply finished unpacking her books onto her desk and turned to me. "So, Missy was just telling me about this Legacy thing. These people sure are big on their exclusivity."

"That's an understatement," I replied, leaning back against my desk.

"It's so annoying. All they can talk about is getting their invitations. It's like they're not even thinking about your party anymore," she said, crossing her arms over her chest.

"My party?" I asked.

"The Billings Masquerade! Don't tell me you've forgotten as well! It was your idea. And a good one, I thought, with the whole fund-raiser thing," she said.

"Oh, well, yeah. But the Legacy means a lot to everyone. I get it," I said, averting my eyes. I picked up a pen from my desk and toyed with it. "Besides, I still plan to set up the scholarship fund in Cheyenne's name. We can start with money from the Billings alumni fund and then ask for donations."

"So you're just going to give up," Sabine said.

"What do you mean?" I asked, stung by her unusually judgmental tone.

"I mean, you should go down there and tell those girls that instead of moping, they should be planning the masquerade. The one they were so excited about," Sabine said, stepping toward me. "You're the president. This was your thing. And now they're ignoring it."

I stared at her, dumbfounded. "Sabine, the Billings Masquerade . . . it was a good idea, but it's not the Legacy. You don't understand what this party means to these people. It's, like, a point of honor. They have to go."

"So that's it. You just back down," Sabine sniffed.

"I'm not backing down. I'm going to help them get into the Legacy," I told her. "Give the people what they want, right?"

"I don't get you. Why are you going to help them get into this thing you can't even go to and help them dismiss your party and your authority in the process?" she asked. "Doesn't that offend you?"

"Okay, when did you become Miss Revolutionary?" I joked, trying to lighten the sudden and extreme tension.

Sabine turned away from me and shook her head. "I'm just trying to help you," she said. "You're the president of Billings. I just wish you would start acting like it."

I felt as if I'd just been slapped across the face. "Well, I think I *am* acting like it. I'm going to get Easton into the Legacy. For Billings, for Easton—"

"For Noelle," she said bitterly.

Ah. So there was the real truth. Noelle. She had a problem with Noelle.

"I'm not doing this for her," I said.

At least not *just* for her.

Sabine gazed at me for a long moment, looking hurt and betrayed. "Whatever you say." She turned around and picked up a book from her desk. She picked at its spine, then hugged it to her chest. "Hey, maybe we can do something together that night—the two of us. Since neither one of us will be able to go," she suggested hopefully.

I wasn't feeling all that buddy-buddy toward her after all the criticism, but I didn't want to hurt her feelings. So I said, "Yeah. Maybe."

But inside I was actually hoping I would find a way to finagle an invite to the Legacy. The very idea of missing out, of having to listen to everyone around me gab about how amazing it was and relate the minor details of everything I'd missed, made me cringe. I was president of Billings. There had to be a way.

"I was just going to walk over to the solarium to get some coffee," Sabine said. "Do you want to—"

At that moment, the door to our room was flung open and Noelle grabbed my arm. "Sorry, Frenchie. Gotta borrow our girl," she said.

Then she dragged me right out of the room, leaving a very dejected-looking Sabine behind.

OSTRACISM

The entire population of Billings, minus Sabine, was gathered in the parlor, nursing coffees, talking in low tones and looking jittery. I felt as if I'd just walked in on an Al-Anon meeting. (I had attended one before, along with my brother, at the urging of my father, who had thought it might help us cope with my mom. It didn't.) They all looked up at me with hopeful, bloodshot eyes.

"All right. I've brought our fearless leader," Noelle said, depositing me in front of the fireplace. She took a step away and turned to me, arms crossed. "We need to figure out what to do about the Legacy," she told me, flipping her dark hair over her shoulder. "Everyone's freaking out."

"Clearly," I replied.

Even Lorna and Astrid looked upset. And, like myself, they wouldn't be getting invites.

"This level of stress is not good for my complexion," Portia said. "I mean, V.N.G."

Very Not Good. I knew that one. There wasn't a zit in sight, but who was I to quibble?

"I just don't get it," London pouted, tugging on her hair. "Why did everyone get them but us? What did *we* do?"

"I didn't do anything," Vienna volunteered, quite unnecessarily.

"Whoever's throwing it must have a grudge against Easton or something," Tiffany said, snapping a photo of Kiki's boots, which Astrid had painted with swirls of orange and yellow paint during their art class that day. "It's the only explanation."

"Unless the Easton stack of invites just got lost in the mail," Rose offered hopefully as she tugged on her red curls.

"Still, somebody would have gotten one," I said. "And apparently none of our alumni have received them either."

Noelle shot me a "how did you know that?" look that made my toes curl. I wouldn't be answering that question any time soon.

"Omigod! Even the grads have been blackballed? What are we going to do?" London wailed. There was a general grumble and a few sighs of despair. Enough was enough already.

"Okay, look. I have an idea," I announced, silencing the room. "We need to get our hands on one of the invitations. If we can do that, maybe we can figure out where they came from. And if we can figure out where they came from, we can find out who bought them."

"Good idea!" Tiffany announced. *"Very CSI."*

I grinned. "So . . . get dialing. You all know someone who got one. Get somebody to send us an original."

A dozen cell phones flipped open. Texts were rapidly typed and sent. A few people made actual calls. Of those few, we could all instantly tell the news wasn't good.

"No way. No way!" Vienna half screeched. She stood up and removed the phone from her ear, the better to yell into the receiver. "You suck, Vanessa! I hope you choke on a condom and die!" she shouted, slapping the phone closed.

"Vienna!" Rose admonished.

"What? We all know my sister's a slut," Vienna said with wide-eyed innocence.

Her sister? That was kind of the pot calling the kettle black, wasn't it? I wondered why Vanessa Clark didn't go to Easton, but let that impertinent question pass.

"What happened?" I asked.

"She said, and I quote, 'I can't send you the invitation,'" Vienna said, putting on an overly shrill voice and tipping her head from side to side, like a little girl mocking someone on the playground. "'I just got an e-mail saying that if anyone shared info about the Legacy with an Easton student, the planner would find out about it, and the person who blabbed would be kept out.' Ugh! I am so not giving her Bubbles now."

"Bubbles?"

"My horse," Vienna mumbled.

Her horse. The best hand-me-down Scott had ever given me was a portable CD player.

"You guys? Rourke says the same thing!" London cried, clutching her phone with both hands as she read a text. "He's afraid of the e-mail."

"That's what they're all saying," Kiki confirmed, kicking back on the sofa and crossing her now colorful combat boots on the table with a bang. She tipped her head back to look up at the ceiling and her pink bangs fell back from her face. "If Vanessa isn't getting your horse, can I have him?" she asked the ceiling.

Vienna looked like she was actually pondering this, but the rest of the room was on high alert. I looked at Noelle. Clearly this ostracism went far beyond anything I could have possibly imagined. For once, my baffled expression was mirrored in her own. For once, Noelle Lange did not know what was going on. That realization was the most disturbing of all.

A CHALLENGE

"Whit is losing it. He thinks the world as we know it is crumbling,"
Constance whispered to me during morning services on Tuesday.
"According to him, this Legacy snubbing is an affront against every-
thing it stands for."

Like what? Drugs? Random sex acts? Underage drinking?

Not that I was getting all goody-goody, but it was kind of funny
how old-world honor had somehow devolved into getting an invite to
the biggest night of debauchery known to man.

"And I was going to get to go this year as his plus one," Constance
mumbled, looking down at her hands. "It figures."

I gnawed on the inside of my lip. There was a general sense of dis-
gruntled acceptance on campus this morning. I had spent half the
night poring over the Billings info, trying to come up with a plan of
attack, and I had a few ideas. But if people were starting to accept the
fact that we weren't going to the Legacy, then maybe I'd be better off

dropping it. Did I really want to bother some illustrious alumni with a petty, whining query about a party? Did I really want my first act as Billings president to be that superficial? Maybe Sabine was right. Maybe I'd be better off going back to my original plan and throwing a masquerade in Cheyenne's honor. There was something more honorable in that. More mature and forward thinking. I was starting to think that the Billings Masquerade would make a much better first impression on the alumni committee. Plus there was the added bonus of me actually being able to attend. And of maybe, somehow, proving Cheyenne's final e-mail wrong.

"Before you are dismissed, I have one final announcement to make," Headmaster Cromwell said, taking the podium. He wore a dark blue suit and a yellow tie, pinned, as always, with an American flag tie tack. His white hair was slicked back from his square face and his eyes slid over the chapel with obvious disdain. Why had a man who clearly detested teenagers ever taken a job like this? "I am aware that the annual Legacy party is scheduled, as always, for the end of this month."

The chapel filled with the sounds of creaking pews and surprised murmurs. No adult, as far as I knew, had ever avowed any knowledge of the Legacy to the students. It was the ultimate "don't ask, don't tell." The headmaster rapped his knuckles against the podium to get our attention. The sound echoed ominously through the high-ceilinged chapel, and silence fell.

"I am also aware that previous administrations have looked the other way when it comes to this particular event, caring not for the safety of our students, nor for the reputation of this academy," Cromwell continued, his voice even more stern than usual. "That ignorance ends with me."

There was no sound in the chapel other than my own breathing. Which was starting to grow shallow. I hated this man. I so, *so* hated him. First he'd dismantled every Billings tradition he could get his hands on, then he'd interrogated us all into the wee hours of the morning on the night of initiation and expelled Cheyenne. Which, of course, had seemed like a blessing, after everything Cheyenne had done. It had seemed like the end of a nightmare. But in twenty-twenty hindsight, it had only meant the beginning of a new one. Now this.

"If anyone attempts to leave this campus on the night of October thirty-first, rest assured that I will know about it, that those persons will be stopped, and that the punishment will be severe," Cromwell said ominously. "This is my school. I make the rules. You are to follow them."

Was I just imagining it, or did he look right at me when he said that? I felt my heart flutter with defiance. Was he challenging me? Daring me?

"You are dismissed," Cromwell said.

The school rose as one and filed into the aisles.

"What a dick," someone behind me said.

"Obviously the ignorance *didn't* end with him if he doesn't even know about the invites."

"Like he could really stop us from going. If we wanted to get out, we'd get out."

"I really don't like this guy," Noelle said as I joined her.

"Yeah. Tell me about it," I said.

I shoved past her into the bright autumn sun, feeling adrenaline pumping through my veins. I had always hated being told what to do. The only time I had ever really tolerated it was last year, when I had been trying to get into Billings, but even then it had been difficult. Now, I found, I hated even more being told what I couldn't do. The mystery planner was trying to keep us out of the Legacy, and now Cromwell was making it his own personal mission to thwart us, too. Who did these people think they were? Easton had as much right to participate in the Legacy as anyone.

"Oh, well. Looks like the poor Billings Girls are going to miss out on the biggest party of the year," Ivy Slade said, giving us a fake pout as she strolled by. "Whatever will you write in your diaries that night?"

My fingers curled into fists. What the hell did this girl have against us?

"Welcome back, Noelle," she said with obvious distaste. "Killed anyone lately?"

A klatch of junior guys overheard this and paused to cackle at the joke, waiting for Noelle's reaction. My stomach clenched. Ivy needed to go. Seriously.

"No. But I can be tempted," Noelle replied.

Ivy snorted a laugh, but wisely turned around and sauntered off. So did her audience, looking suddenly wan.

"God. Who let that girl back in?" Noelle said under her breath. Quite ironically, I thought.

"I cannot believe Cromwell issued an ultimatum about the Legacy," Missy said at my shoulder. Most of the other Billings Girls had gathered behind Noelle and me just outside the chapel doors. "I mean, seriously. Like he hasn't done enough already."

She was, of course, referring to his supposed role in Cheyenne's suicide.

"But this is a good thing, no?" Sabine asked. "We will definitely hold the Billings Masquerade now."

I turned around slowly, my jaw clenched. Everyone was watching me, waiting for my signal.

"No," I said tersely. Between Cromwell, Ivy, and whoever this mystery Legacy planner was, there were a lot of people whom I wanted to see eat crow right about then. "Easton is going to the Legacy. No matter what I have to do to get us in."

RESPECT

I was officially pissed off. And when I'm pissed off, I take action. So in the fifteen-minute break between lunch and history class, when most of the school was enjoying the warm autumn day on the quad, sucking down lattes, or cramming for quizzes, I stole back to Billings and went to work.

The night before, I'd had a bit of an epiphany while reading through the alumni files. Several Billings alums had children who had chosen to go to other private schools. Places like Choate or Barton or Chapin—often, the schools their fathers had attended. Some of these alums had family lineages listed, and next to each family member—dating back generations—was the name of the school from which he or she had graduated. This was the information that was most useful. Because if a Billings alum was married to, say, a Barton man whose father had also gone to Barton and whose child now went to Barton . . . then that child would be invited to the Legacy. After an hour of searching, I had come up with a list of Billings alums whose kids had, without a doubt, already received invitations to the Legacy, thanks to their fathers' lines.

With not much time to spare, I sprinted up to my room, grabbed the list, and chose the name right at the top. Jenna Korman, CEO of Posh Cosmetics, one of the biggest upscale cosmetics companies in the country. Considering her stature, I was fairly certain she wouldn't have time to take my call, but I had to try. I grabbed my cell phone and dialed the number.

"Posh Cosmetics, Ms. Korman's office," a clipped voice answered on the first ring.

"Yeah, hi, I'm calling for Ms. Korman. I'm from—"

"I'm sorry. Ms. Korman is unavailable at the moment," the woman said, clearly annoyed. "I can take a message."

Dammit. My skin burned, realizing how unprofessional I must have sounded.

"Oh. Okay. My name is Reed Brennan. I'm calling from—"

"Oh. Miss Brennan. I apologize. I'll put you right through," the voice said, turning suddenly warm.

I blinked, feeling like I'd just slipped through Alice's looking glass. What was that? Was she kidding? And why had she acted like she knew my name?

"Reed Brennan. This is a pleasant surprise," a throaty voice said in my ear. "What can I do for you?"

"I—is this Jenna Korman?" I asked, stunned.

"Yes, it is. How is everything at Easton these days?" she asked pleasantly. "I trust you're all recovering. Such a tragedy. Cheyenne Martin was a real asset to the house and the school."

"Yes . . . yes, she was," I said. This was so not what I had been expecting. "We're . . . fine, I guess."

"Good. Now, is there something I can help you with?" Ms. Korman asked.

"Actually, yes," I said, clearing my throat. I didn't want to waste any more of her time than I had to. "For some reason Easton has been shut out of the Legacy this year."

"Yes, I've heard grumblings to that effect," she said bitterly.

"Well, I'm trying to figure out why, so I can fix the problem," I told her. "But I need to get my hands on one of the actual invitations. I hear that your daughter goes to Hotchkiss and that she might—"

"Not a problem. I'll call home right now and have our butler FedEx it right to you," Ms. Korman said.

Butler? Of course she had a butler.

"Will overnight suffice, or do you need it sooner? I could have my driver bring it up to you this afternoon if need be."

A laugh bubbled up in my throat, but I choked it back. Where were the white rabbit and the Mad Hatter? Shouldn't I be getting some tea about now? "No, thank you. Tomorrow will be fine. Thank you so much, Ms. Korman."

"Please. It's Jenna. No need to thank me. That's why we're here," she replied. "And congratulations, Reed. We're all proud to have you assume the presidency."

"Thank you," I replied.

"Good-bye."

There was a click and the connection died, but I sat there holding the phone for a good ten seconds more. I could not believe that had worked. Could not believe how easy it had been. She had known who I was. Her assistant had known who I was. And just like that, I was in. I started to understand what being president of Billings really meant. Open doors, answered calls . . . respect.

I turned and pulled out my desk chair, removing the Chloé bag. It had been hidden there since the night I'd received it. I opened it up, took out the Neiman Marcus catalog, and started shoving my things inside the leathery softness.

I hadn't really realized it before, but until this moment, I had felt unworthy of carrying the bag.

Not anymore.

SPECIAL TALENTS

I raced down the soccer field opposite Noelle on Wednesday afternoon, Bernadette Baskin right on my heels. The sun was just starting to dip behind the trees, which meant that at any second, Coach Lisick would call practice, and I wanted to score before she blew the whistle. I needed to score.

Forcing a burst of energy, I surged ahead suddenly, leaving Bernadette in my dust. With barely a glance, Noelle saw I was open and passed me the ball. A perfect, gunshot pass, so fast the center had no chance of catching up to it. As I approached the goal I looked left, and Astrid, who for some reason Lisick had decided to try out in goal, totally went for it. She jumped to her right, vaulting herself into the air, and I easily jammed the ball into the far corner of the net.

"Yes!" Noelle cheered, pumping her fist.

We jogged across the pitch to meet in the center and slapped hands and hugged. If it was good to have Noelle back at Billings, it was almost as good to have her back on the team. We needed her aggressive play. No one on the field was her equal.

"All right, ladies! Nice practice!" Coach Lisick called out after a bleat on her whistle. "Come get a drink and then hit the showers!

"Solid effort," Astrid said, jogging over to join us. She had tied her short black hair up in two ponytails that stuck straight up from her head like antennae. "You do know I gave you that last one, right?" she joked.

"That British wit slays me," Noelle said with a wry smile. She hooked her arm heavily over my shoulders. "So, did you get it?"

"Oh, I got it," I replied.

"Got what?" Astrid asked.

"The Legacy invite," I whispered. "It's in my bag."

"Well, let's have it, then!" Astrid cried.

"Shh! Not here. On the way back to Billings," I replied.

At the water jug we were joined by Sabine, who, after displaying an inherent fear of the ball and a complete lack of speed during her first few practices, had been appointed equipment manager. She handed me and Astrid paper cups, ignoring Noelle, who rolled her eyes and grabbed her own, filling it to the brim. I bit my tongue to keep from saying anything to Sabine, but I was going to have to make her understand one of these days. Noelle was not a person you wanted to mess with. Or shun. No matter how she treated you.

"Nice goal," Sabine said to me with a smile. "No offense," she added to Astrid.

"None taken," Astrid replied.

"Let's go," Noelle said crumpling her cup and launching it at the garbage can. "I want to see this thing."

"Wait. Let's help Sabine clean up first and carry the stuff down," I said.

"Reed, come on. Frenchie can handle it," Noelle said as if Sabine weren't even there. "It *is* her job."

My face burned on Sabine's behalf. Maybe Josh was right about Noelle creating drama. Sabine had never done a thing to offend her. The girl was completely innocuous. And yet Noelle seemed determined to make her feel like some poseur geek who didn't belong.

"It's all right. You two go. I'll help Sabine," Astrid offered.

"Aw! Isn't that sweet? Britain and France, working together! It's all so United Nations I could cry." Noelle put her arm around me again. "Now let's go." She forcibly swung me around and headed for the hill. I barely had time to grab my duffel bag before she dragged me off. "Where is it?" she asked, eyeing my bag greedily.

"Okay, okay. God, I'd hate to see you on Christmas morning," I replied. I pulled out the opened FedEx envelope and extracted the thick, ivory card. I had already inspected it at every chance I could for the last four hours, but the only thing even remotely interesting about it was the imprint of an orchid on the back. Other than that, there were no markings whatsoever. Not a company name, nothing.

"Well. This is helpful," Noelle said sarcastically, handing it back to me with disgust, like it was a used tissue.

"I know. But I figure the orchid has to mean something," I told her. "And I have an idea who might know."

"Interesting," Noelle said with a teasing smile. "One thing I always loved about you, Reed—you never were a quitter."

I smiled as we opened the door to Billings. As usual at this time of day, London, Vienna, and a few of the other girls were hanging out in the parlor. I walked in and dropped my bags, still holding on to the invite.

"London, can I talk to you for a sec?" I asked.

Her eyes widened when she saw me, and she yanked the earbuds from her ears. "Is that it!?" She jumped up from her seat, tripped over Kiki's legs, and almost fell into me. "Let me see! Let me see!"

She snatched the invite from my hands as the other girls gathered around her to peek over her shoulders. After reading over the info we had all long since memorized, she flipped the card over. Her finger traced the outline of the orchid and she smiled.

"Bouquet. This invitation came from Bouquet," she said.

I knew it. I knew she would know. Everyone had her special talents. Even the Twin Cities.

"In Boston?" Rose asked.

"The one and only," London said triumphantly, handing the card back to me. "They have all these different levels of card stock and design, and they imprint each invitation with a flower according to its price point. Orchid is the highest. Whoever bought these has some bank."

Shocker.

"You know exactly where this place is?" I asked.

London rolled her eyes. "Please. I'll get you the address and digits right now."

She reached into her Bottega Veneta bag and pulled out her red Treo. After hitting a few buttons, she smiled. "Just zapped it to you."

On cue, my iPhone beeped. I looked at Noelle. "So, Boston, huh?"

Noelle grinned in response. "Road trip!"

SELFISH

"We should make a day of it," Noelle said as we sat down to breakfast Thursday morning. "Brunch at Azure, then some detective work, and then shopping. If we're going to the Legacy, we're going to need some couture."

She tucked her plaid mini under her thighs and sat in the chair that had, until her return, been my chair. I sat down across from her, in Ariana's regular seat. Either Josh or Sabine had been sitting here most of this year. Which had made it seem friendly again. But for some reason, in that chair, I just felt awkward.

"You're forgetting something," I said, attempting to focus. I picked up the top half of my bagel to spread some cream cheese.

"Like what?" she demanded. Like her forgetting something was unheard of.

"I won't be going. Even if we fix the problem, I don't get an invite," I told her.

She shrugged, waving her knife in the air. "So? We'll find some-one with a plus one to take you. We did it last year."

"But last year I wasn't with Josh," I replied. Technically I was "with" Thomas. Or so I had thought. But I had gone with Whit, because every-one had told me Thomas would be at the Legacy, and I needed to see him. Little did any of us know that, at that point, Thomas had already been dead for weeks. Rotting somewhere, alone in the woods, dead and cold and—

Okay. I wasn't thinking about that. Not now.

This chair was bad for my psyche.

"I can't just go with someone else," I finished.

"Reed. This is about getting in. Not about how you get in," Noelle said, in that tone that used to make me feel small. It still did, but not quite *as* small. "Once you're there, you can hang out with your ball and chain as much as you want."

I smirked. "So, how are we going to get to Boston?" I asked, attempt-ing to focus. "I mean, even if we do get a pass from Cromwell . . . do we need to hire a car or something?

"No. I have a car," Noelle said, taking a dainty bite of her bagel.

"You have a car. On campus?" I asked, incredulous.

"That was a total deal-breaker for Daddy in his negotiations with the Crom," she said blithely.

I laughed. "The Crom. That makes him sound like a robot or something."

"Well, he kind of is, no?" Noelle said, raising her brows as she bit into her bagel. "Anyway, don't worry. I've got the passes covered."

"Passes for what?" Josh asked, kissing me hello as he joined us. He dropped his tray full of doughnuts, sugar cereal, and coffee on the table, removed his battered corduroy jacket with its plaid elbow patches—a look only he could pull off—and draped it on the back of his chair. Underneath was a plain, long-sleeved white waffle tee with tiny paint spatters on one side.

"For Saturday," Noelle told him. "Reed and I are going on a road trip."

Josh dropped into his seat hard. "No, you're not," he said, surprised.

"Yeah. We're going to Boston to check out the store where the Legacy invites came from. We're gonna see if we can find out who bought them," I told him, taking a sip of my juice.

"Nice. Want me to come? I can bring down the hurt if you need it," Gage offered, straddling a chair.

"That won't be necessary," Noelle replied, rolling her eyes.

Josh turned fully in his seat to face me as the other chairs at the table started to fill up with my housemates. His blue eyes were serious. "Reed, aren't you forgetting something?" he asked, his voice low.

My brows knit as I looked at him. I was a total blank. "What?

"We're supposed to go to Maine on Saturday. The reunion?"

I felt like someone had just let all the air out of a balloon, right into my face. I was an idiot. A complete and total idiot. I hadn't thought about the Hollis family reunion since I'd scribbled the date down in my English notebook Monday night. There had just been so many other things going on, I had completely spaced.

"Oh my God, Josh. I'm so sorry. I totally forgot," I said, feeling suddenly warm. Everyone was watching us. I could feel it. Josh must have felt it too, because he leaned in closer to me, ducking his face behind mine, as if to hide from Gage.

"You have to come. I told my whole family you were going to be there," he said.

"I know, but . . . Josh, this is huge," I told him, pleading. "This is about saving the Legacy. Everyone at Easton is counting on this."

Josh pulled back a little and looked me in the eye. I had never seen him look so hurt. "What about me? I'm counting on you too."

There was a lump in my throat that was threatening to choke me. I felt awful. I did. But didn't he get how important this was? As president of Billings, this was practically my job. I'd promised everyone I'd fix the situation. If I went back on that now, I'd look like a total flake and a failure, and I'd *just* gotten the job. Besides, the Hollises had this party every year. It wasn't like this would be my only chance to go.

"Yeah, but even you said there would be hundreds of people there," I reminded him. "No one's going to notice if I'm not. You'll be fine."

"Dude, grow a pair," Gage said loudly. "This is the Legacy we're talking about. If Backwater Brennan's gonna save it, I say let her save it. I mean, how selfish can you be?"

Josh stared at me. He was waiting for me to back down. I knew he was. But I couldn't. I wouldn't. And as guilty as I felt about the reunion, I was irritated that he wanted me to go. On some level Gage was right. If we were going to figure this out before Halloween, every moment counted. It was this weekend or nothing. If I didn't fix this, all the Easton legacies were screwed. Didn't he see that?

Dash would have seen it. He would have understood.

Something shifted in Josh's eyes and he pulled away. "Fine. Whatever. I guess I can just tell them you're sick."

"That's the spirit, Hollis," Gage said, offering his fist for a bump. Josh ignored it and took a bite of a doughnut instead.

"Don't worry, Josh. I'll take good care of our girl," Noelle said teasingly.

The wrong person saying the exact wrong thing. Josh shoved the rest of the doughnut in his mouth at once and didn't speak again for the rest of the meal.

BOUQUET

Noelle's on-campus car was a slick silver Mercedes convertible with soft leather seats. With the top down, our sunglasses on, and her satellite radio blasting, we caught more than a few intrigued stares as we zoomed along the highway to Boston.

With day passes from our art history teacher to check out the Gauguin exhibit at the MFA, we had the entire day to do whatever we wanted. All we had to do was pop into the museum and pick up a map and some badges to prove that we'd been there, and we'd even get extra credit for the day. Noelle was an evil genius.

And best of all, when I'd checked my e-mail the night before, there had been no sign of Cheyenne's note from beyond the grave. It was over. I was truly free.

After an incredible breakfast at Azure, a restaurant in a swank hotel in the heart of Boston, we walked to Bouquet. It was a beautiful, sunny day—the air clear and crisp with anticipation. I had never been to Boston in the daylight, and I found it even more beautiful than I could have imagined. The skinny, crooked streets; the ancient brick buildings; the old-fashioned torch street lamps; the gold plates on various buildings, outlining their rich histories. Washington slept here. Jefferson ate there. Soon I found myself in a quaint shopping district where eager shoppers popped in and out of pristine shops filled with autumn clothes and winter coats. I had eaten so much I felt like I was in a food coma as I followed Noelle along the packed sidewalk. Not an easy scene to navigate on four mimosas, but I managed not to knock anyone over, I think. Taking a deep breath, I just felt free. It was good to be away from Easton and Billings and all the pressure and guilt. I knew it was traitorous, but I couldn't help feeling that I had already had more fun than I would have had all day at the Hollis family reunion.

Of course, the instant this occurred to me, I felt guilty and wanted to call Josh and see how it was going, but I had a feeling my reception would be a cool one. And besides, we had just reached the door of Bouquet.

"This is it," Noelle said, pushing her sunglasses up into her hair. "Let me do the talking."

"No problem," I said. And burped. How much champagne had been in those mimosas anyway?

"Classy," Noelle said, scrunching her nose. She opened the door to the tiny shop, and bells tinkled overhead. Inside the sunlit store, the atmosphere was hushed. Along the lemon yellow walls were shallow shelves displaying all sorts of colorful stationery sets, thank-you cards, and party invitations. Tall tables along the center of the room were bursting with fresh flowers in all the colors of the season: red roses, orange lilies, yellow daisies. At the back of the store were four long wooden tables, where a mother and daughter sat, poring over huge books of sample invitations. The woman helping them whispered her suggestions and instructions. This place felt like a museum itself. Maybe we wouldn't have to hit the MFA after all.

"Can I help you?" a squat saleslady behind the counter asked.

She was practically wedged into her gray suit, and her dark hair was pulled back in a low ponytail. She wore no jewelry and, after giving us a quick once-over, didn't look very pleased at the prospect of dealing with a pair of teenagers. Noelle cleared her throat and stepped forward, and I was suddenly more than grateful for her presence. I hated dealing with snooty salespeople. Back home in Croton, I was sometimes too intimidated to even walk into the Gap.

"Yes. We're trying to find out who ordered this invitation," Noelle said, sliding the Legacy invite across the tall wooden counter.

The woman picked it up, turned it over for a cursory glance, then placed it down again. She used all four fingertips to slide it determinedly back to Noelle.

"Sorry. All orders are confidential," she sniffed.

Noelle looked the woman up and down, and for a brief moment I thought she was going to raise holy hell, but then she smiled. She smiled the most genuine smile I'd ever seen from Noelle before in my life.

"I understand," she said. "It's just . . . these girls at our school?" she said, gesturing at me over her shoulder. "They're throwing this exclusive party, and they're purposely leaving out all these other girls, you know? Just because they're, like, a little chunky or have bad skin or come from the wrong families. It's, like, totally arbitrary."

It was all I could do not to laugh. Noelle was doing a pitch-perfect imitation of Constance. Sweet, innocent Constance Talbot. Her own polar opposite. I had to turn away so the woman wouldn't notice the reddening of my face.

"That's awful!" the woman lamented, suddenly sympathetic.

Unbelievable. In ten seconds Noelle had read this woman perfectly and knew exactly what would make her crack.

"All we want to do is find out which girl is really orchestrating all this so that we can, you know, confront her," Noelle continued pleadingly as I looked over my shoulder. "It's so unfair."

The woman looked Noelle and me up and down. "Hang on. You two weren't invited?" she asked suspiciously.

My heart skipped a beat. Clearly she had read Noelle right back. She was far too gorgeous and well dressed ever to be ostracized based on looks or money.

"No, no. We were invited," Noelle said, turning her eyes down modestly. "That's why we have the invitation. It's just a lot of our friends were left out, and it's not like we'd go without them. We want to stand up to this girl on their behalf. There *is* a little thing called loyalty, you know?"

The woman still looked unconvinced. This wasn't going to work after all. Then Noelle leaned into the counter and looked earnestly into the woman's eyes.

"Look, two years ago, I never would have been invited. We're talking glasses, bad skin, overbite. Not a pretty sight."

I didn't believe any of that for a second, but she painted an interesting picture.

"I know how it feels to be left out, and I'm just trying to make sure it doesn't happen to anyone I care about," Noelle continued. "So can you help us?"

The saleslady checked the back of the room, where her colleague was still engrossed.

"Okay. But if anyone asks, you didn't get this from me," she said.

She turned to her computer and quickly typed in some information. I rejoined Noelle at the counter, amazed. She held out her hand to me, behind her and out of sight, and I quickly swiped my own palm across it.

"Ah, yes. I took this order myself," the woman whispered. "I remember this girl. Blond, thin, blue eyes. About your age, I'd say. She had this sort of odd, detached way about her. Sound familiar?"

A chill shot right through me. Noelle and I looked at each other. Yes, it sounded familiar. But it couldn't possibly be.

Noelle cleared her throat. "Maybe," she said. "Do you have her name?"

"Yes. It was—" The woman leaned toward us and lowered her voice until it was barely audible. "Amanda Hold."

Noelle's eyes lit up, and she bit back a smirk. Did she know this girl? "Do you remember anything else?" she asked. "Was anyone with her? Or did she call anyone while she was here?

"Actually, yes," the woman said, speaking in a more normal voice. "I remember she told someone on the phone that she was going to Ungari Jewelers later that day."

Noelle slipped the invite back into her bag. "Thank you so much, Miss . . . ?"

"Roxanne," the woman said, reaching her hand out to shake Noelle's. "I hope this Amanda girl gets what's coming to her."

Noelle smiled again, this time looking more like herself. "Oh, she will. Don't worry. We'll make sure of that."

OUR TURN

"Nice work," I said to Noelle as we walked along Commonwealth.

"Like taking veggies away from a big, fat baby," she replied with a smirk.

Okay, rude. But whatever. The phrase "taking candy from a baby" had never made sense to me anyway. Wouldn't that be *hard* to do? "So who's Amanda Hold? You know her?"

Noelle laughed. "Reed, please. Amanda Hold?" She looked at me in a leading way. I stared back. "A. Man. To. Hold? Amanda Hold? It's one of the oldest aliases in the book."

"Oh," I said, feeling stupid. "Why would someone use a fake name at a stationer?"

A twist of dread knotted up my stomach as I recalled Roxanne's description of Amanda. She had described Ariana perfectly. And of all people, Ariana had good reasons to make up a name. But no, it wasn't possible. Ariana was locked up in a mental institution somewhere, wasn't she? Locked up for life.

"Stop thinking what you're thinking," Noelle said firmly. "There are a million blond-haired, blue-eyed girls with blank stares in this world. It's a cliché for a reason. And Ariana is safely tucked away in her padded cell. Though it's probably padded with Prada."

She swung open a large, silver door to a stately looking shop. I hesitated for a moment before following. It was the first time she had directly mentioned Ariana—her former best friend—since she'd retuned to Easton, and it brought up a zillion questions. But as a Hulk-size security guard stared me down from just inside the door, now didn't seem like the time to ask.

"In or out, miss?" he said to me gruffly.

"In. I'm in," I replied.

Inside, the air was crisply cool, and everything was gray. Gray carpeting, gray walls, gray felt inside hundreds of gleaming glass cases. Everywhere I looked there were diamonds. Diamonds, rubies, emeralds, sapphires, amethysts, and on and on. In one case there was a pink diamond the size of a quarter set into an ornate necklace of tiny white diamonds set to look like a string of flowers. Thousands of diamonds. I couldn't imagine wearing something that exquisite and expensive on my neck. I'd have to take Krav Maga classes first or I'd never feel safe.

"Reed. Look at this." Noelle waved me over. "Third one from the back." Her fingertip hovered over the case, making no contact between skin and glass. She was pointing to a square-cut diamond, gorgeous, huge, set high on a ring of pinpoint-size diamonds that lined the entire band. I swallowed back the sudden taste of acid in my throat. Engagement rings. She was looking at engagement rings.

I surreptitiously glanced at her profile. Her eyes were bright, her expression almost dreamy. Was she thinking of Dash? Why did the very idea make me ill?

"Can I help you, ladies? Perhaps take something out for you?" The elderly gentleman behind the counter spoke in a hushed baritone. Apparently rich people really liked quiet in their stores.

Noelle started to speak, but I put a hand on her arm to stop her. One, because I was partially scared she was, in fact, going to start trying on engagement rings. Two, because if she was going to try to work the guy, I wanted my chance first. This was, after all, supposed to be my mission. Not hers.

"I'm Amanda Hold," I told him. "I placed an order a couple weeks back and I just wanted to check on the status."

"Of course, Ms. Hold. This way," he said with a nod.

We followed him to a computer tucked away in a corner. Apparently I could get over my fear of salespeople when I was feeling territorial.

A few keystrokes and "my" order popped up. "Yes. I see we have three hundred and twenty-five platinum money clips on order for you, as well as four hundred and seven gold rings. All etched with a single L."

My throat was dry. This was it. The Legacy token. This so-called Amanda girl was really running the show.

"Yes. That's right," I managed to say.

"They should all be delivered to the address you provided within the week," he told me with a kind smile.

The address! Perfect! That was all we needed.

"And what—"

This time Noelle's hand on my arm stopped me. "You wanted to add to the order, didn't you, Amanda?" she said pointedly. She reached into her bag and pulled out a tiny piece of paper on which some numbers were scribbled. "We'll need fifty-three more money clips and sixty-five rings," Noelle said. "And I'll be paying for those myself. Amanda's already done enough," she added with a bright smile.

"Of course," the man said with another nod. "If I could just get your credit card and delivery information, Miss . . . ?"

"Lange. Noelle Lange," Noelle replied, slapping down her American Express Black.

Once the order was placed and we were back out in the fresh air, I realized my near mistake. Amanda Hold wouldn't have had to ask the guy for her own address. I'd almost given us away. I was really going to have to work on my undercover talents. Or at least not go on these missions after four mimosas.

"So, why fifty-three and sixty-five?" I asked Noelle as we strolled up Commonwealth again.

"That should cover current legacies and young alumni. Plus all the Billings Girls," Noelle said matter-of-factly. She tucked a lock of hair behind her ear that had been tossed free by a cool breeze. "You're welcome."

"What?" I blurted. "You didn't."

"I did. I take care of my own," she said, lacing her arm through mine. She casually checked out a window display as we strolled by.

"I can't believe you're going to mess with the Legacy rules."

Noelle paused and looked me in the eye. "This Amanda Hold person messed with them first," she said, slipping her dark sunglasses over her eyes. "Now it's our turn."

OFF AGAIN

The shop was called Flourish, and it was so exclusive it was marked only by a gold plate on the brick outer wall that listed its address and 1912 as its date of establishment. Walking through the door, I felt as if a net were going to fall from the ceiling and trap me while alarms blared, signaling that a poseur had crossed the threshold. No matter how much time I spent in places like this, I still felt as if I didn't totally belong. But instead of sounding the alarm, the black-suited salesladies rushed forward across the deep, plush carpeting, offering champagne, coffee, and a guided tour through the collections. Less than an hour later, Noelle and I were settled in a dressing room bigger than my bedroom back home, with twelve gowns apiece to try on, each more exquisite than the last.

But first, the torture.

The seamstress had Noelle's measurements on file, but mine had to be taken. So a white-haired lady wielding a brown tape measure told me in a clipped tone to strip down to my underwear, and was now in the process of measuring every inch of my half-naked body with her cold, bony fingers.

"God, Reed, I forgot what a prude you are," Noelle said, standing there with her ample breasts perfectly shaped by a black lace bra. Barely covering her butt were black lace boy shorts that made even me blush. "It's not like you have anything to see."

I would have been offended if she hadn't been so right on. Genetics and a predisposition for sports had combined to give me a figure that was more boyish than girlish—broad shoulders, flat stomach, nonexistent hips. At least my boobs had grown a little this year. I had actually shrieked with delight over the summer when Natasha and I had gone shopping and I'd found I'd graduated to a B cup. She'd laughed for about an hour over my reaction.

"Thanks a lot," I said flatly.

Noelle just rolled her eyes. She stepped into a full-skirted black taffeta gown and zipped it up, then gathered the excess fabric of the bodice behind her, defining her perfect hourglass body.

"Don't worry," she said as I winced at the woman's touch. "It'll all be worth it when your gown fits like it was made for you. Because it will be! Darla is a genius."

"Thank you, Miss Lange," Darla said. She crouched in front of me and measured up the side of my bare leg. A ticklish skitter raced along the inside of my thigh, and I almost kicked the poor woman in the head on reflex.

"Sorry," I said as she noticed my wince. She merely pursed her lips and stood.

"All right, Miss Brennan," Darla said. "We're all set. Let us know if you need anything."

"Thank you."

As she strolled out with her clipboard and tape measure, I finally breathed freely again. Noelle grabbed a bronze-colored dress from my selections on the wall.

"This is the one. I know it."

I stepped into the dress, the silky fabric tickling my ankles as it swished around, and slipped my arms through the cap sleeves. I had to gather a lot more fabric behind me than Noelle did. We looked at our reflections in the mirror and I sighed. Next to Noelle, I looked like a ten-year-old playing dress-up.

"Gorgeous. Look what that does for your coloring!" Noelle gushed.

"I don't know. I think I want something more sophisticated," I said as I wrangled my way out of the dress.

"And I want something sexier," Noelle agreed.

She let the gown drop to the ground and kicked it aside, where it joined two other discards. Classic Noelle. The frock was worth thousands and she was using it as a soccer ball. She took down a long, slinky red dress and pulled that on next. I went with a gray strapless with a tiered, feathered skirt. It looked like something Rinnan Hearst, Cheyenne's famous, Oscar-nominated stepmother, might have worn on the red carpet.

"Now *this* is a look," Noelle said, striking a sultry pose in the mirror.

It was all I could do not to gawk. It was a look all right. A breasty, curvy, sexpot look. She pulled all her hair over one shoulder and pursed her lips. She made me think of those pictures of old-school movie vixens like Veronica Lake or Marilyn Monroe.

"You need that dress," I said, zipping up my own.

"I know. Dash will die," she replied.

I jerked and caught my skin in the zipper. Wincing, I yanked it down again and flung myself around to check my back. There was an angry red mark, but I hadn't broken the skin.

"Dash is going to the Legacy?" I asked, keeping my voice even as I rubbed at the red mark, which only made it worse. Hadn't he just told me he and Noelle were not together? Hadn't she said the same that night in New York? What the hell had happened to that?

"Well, yeah," Noelle said, twisting her hair up and holding it behind her head. She turned her face from side to side to inspect. "He's always my plus one. But since it seems even I'm not on the list this year, I just ordered one extra money clip for him."

Wow. She was just breaking rules all over the place, wasn't she?

"Oh."

I finished zipping up the dress and checked my reflection. The gown was gorgeous, with subtle little sparkles trailing across the strapless neckline and down only one side of the bodice, into the feathery skirt. It was sophisticated, definitely. A work of art. But I felt like a troll next to Noelle.

Dash *was* going to die when he saw her. Die and go to heaven. I glanced at her reflection as she looked over her shoulder to check the back of the gown. This was my opportunity. My chance to find out how she really felt about him. What she thought the future might bring.

Maybe if I knew for sure that they were getting back together, or at the very least that Noelle definitely still wanted him, I could get past this ridiculous crush already and focus on Josh. The guy I was supposed to be in love with.

I took a deep breath. Yes. This was a good plan. Find out. Move on. Trying to sound as casual as possible, I asked.

"So, do you think you two will get back together?" I adjusted my gown and checked it out disinterestedly, just for good measure.

"Of course," Noelle said without hesitation.

Everything inside of me sank. Fast. "Really?" I blurted.

Her brown eyes flashed. "You sound surprised."

"No. Not at all," I fumbled, my heart pounding. "I'm just . . . I don't know. I don't even know why you broke up in the first place. I wasn't sure if it was the kind of thing you could get past or . . ."

Shut up, Reed. You're just digging a hole for yourself. Less is more. I bit my tongue to keep from rambling further.

Finally, Noelle answered. "Well, you don't know this, since you weren't here, but until last year Dash and I had a very on-again, off-again relationship, but we always, *always* came back to each other. Right now we're off again, but if I have my way . . ."

Here she paused to give me a look that reminded me that she always got her way.

"We'll be on again before the Legacy," she finished, smoothing her hair.

I stared at my reflection in the mirror. Would Dash *die* if he saw me in this? Not likely. But really, what did it matter? Josh would like it. It was just his kind of thing—interesting lines, an original color. A work of art. Josh would definitely appreciate it.

"I'm taking this one," I said, quickly unzipping the gown and stepping out of the skirt.

"Good choice," Noelle said.

"Come on. We still have to pay for this and hit the MFA. We should get going," I said as I impatiently yanked on my jeans.

"Okay. Want me to pay for yours?" Noelle asked as she returned the dress she was buying to its hanger. Unlike the rejects on the floor.

For some reason her offer made my blood boil. "No. Billings has an account here," I said, holding out my hand for her gown. "I'll just put them on that."

Noelle stared at me for a long moment. A moment in which I had no idea, and in fact feared, what she might be thinking. But then, she slowly smiled.

"Now you're getting the hang of it," she said, handing the dress over. She turned back to the mirror as I turned to go. "Don't forget to tell them we need a rush on the alterations."

"Got it," I grumbled as I shoved my way through the door.

You know everything. You have everything. I got it. Believe me. I do.

UNGRATEFUL

"I have the best news!" I cried as I barreled into my room that evening.

I had decided to focus on the positives. And one major positive was having some news that should actually break Sabine out of the weird funk she'd been in lately. Sure, she had seemed anti-Legacy before, but I knew she'd change her mind now that she'd get to go too. She was sitting on her bed with a needle and thread and some kind of fabric stuck into a ring, which she dropped the moment I entered.

"What? What is it?" she asked, sitting up straight.

"What's that?" I asked, pointing. Momentary distraction. It's not every day you see a sixteen-year-old girl doing needlepoint.

"Just something I'm making for my sister." She tucked it away under her pillow as if embarrassed. But then she lifted her chin in a defiant way. "I do embroidery. It's calming."

"Oh. Okay," I said. I placed my Chloé bag on my bed. Sabine really was different from anyone else at Easton. I could only imagine what Portia and the Twin Cities and Noelle would say about such an old-fashioned and completely unglam hobby. But maybe there was something to this calming idea. Sabine always seemed pretty chill to me.

"So? What's your news?" she asked.

Right. My news! I turned to her, practically bubbling over.

"We *all* are going to the Legacy!" I announced.

Sabine's face fell. "Oh."

Not exactly the enthusiastic response I had been looking for.

"You don't understand! This is beyond incredible!" I cried. "Now we don't have to sit here alone while everyone else traipses off to the biggest party of the year! Noelle got rings for all the Billings Girls, so we're all going to crash. It's going to be an insane night. Just wait."

"Rings? What rings?" Sabine asked, sliding to the end of her bed.

"You need these rings to get in. There's always some piece of jewelry you get that proves you were invited. Last year it was a necklace," I told her. "Anyway, Noelle will be getting them any day, and then all we have to do is get the e-mail with the location and we're in."

"Noelle will be getting them," Sabine said pointedly. She dropped her clasped hands between her knees as she looked up at me.

"Yeah. She ordered them," I told her. "Why?"

"*There's* a surprise," she said.

She shoved herself up and went over to her desk, where she started shifting through her books, her back to me. Okay. Now I was getting seriously annoyed. Not only was she not excited about the Legacy—

a party everyone else at Easton would give their left ear to go to—but she was giving me crap about Noelle. Again.

"What is your problem with Noelle?" I asked.

"Nothing," she said.

My fingers clenched. "No. I want to know."

Sabine sighed and her shoulders slumped. "Well, first of all, she's been mean to me since the day she got here."

"You haven't been all that nice to her, either," I replied.

It was lame, I know. Like Noelle really cared how Sabine treated her. But it was true.

"And second of all, she clearly wants the presidency," Sabine added, as if I hadn't spoken.

"What? She does not!" I said with a scoff.

"Reed!" Sabine was wide-eyed, like she couldn't believe I was so blind. "If she doesn't want to be in charge, why has she let you do nothing on your own since she got here? I don't think she ever liked the masquerade idea. She steered everyone toward the Legacy. Now she's getting all of us into this party, making it impossible for us to hold a Halloween ball of our own, and she's the one getting these rings. So all of Easton—and Billings—is going to give her credit for getting them in. She's undermining you at every turn."

I stared at Sabine, stung. It was amazing how she had just twisted everything to make it look how she wanted it to look. But she hadn't been there. She hadn't seen how I'd almost ruined everything at the jeweler and how Noelle had swooped in to save the day. It wasn't pre-meditated. We'd done it all together, off the cuff. Sabine didn't like

Noelle, so she was turning everything the girl did into some kind of plot.

And, okay, maybe Noelle had schemed in the past, but things were different now. "You're wrong about her," I said firmly. "By paying for all those tokens for us, she was doing something unselfish. She was looking out for the rest of us. She didn't do it for herself."

Sabine looked sad as she sighed again. "If you say so."

Then she sat down at her desk and tucked in, turning her back on me for good this time. Frustrated, I crossed my arms over my chest and turned to stare out the window at the darkening blue sky as the lights flicked on all over the Easton grounds. Sabine was wrong. Noelle and I were friends. I felt like her equal more than ever before. Except in those moments when I was reminded of how new I was to all of this—but still. Noelle and I had done the day's work together. I was sure we would take credit for it together.

NEGLECT

"We're going to the Legacy? All of us?" Constance cried. "Oh my God, Reed! You're my hero!"

Now this was the kind of reaction I was looking for. Constance squealed and practically knocked over the café table between us as she attempted to hug me. Her thick hair got caught on my tongue and I pulled it away quickly, trying hard not to gag and offend her. The Drake House boys at the next table shielded their PSPs just in case any coffee went flying.

"Shh!" I admonished nonetheless, glancing around the packed solarium. At every table students whispered, studied, or sneaked kisses over coffee and scones. "We don't want everyone to hear and start thinking they can get in."

"Oh. Right!" Constance whispered.

"Here you go, Constance! They just came out with a fresh batch of chocolate croissants."

A freshman girl whom I recognized as one of Amberly's sidekicks deposited a plastic plate on our table. Constance looked up at her, nonplussed.

"Uh, thanks . . . Lara, right?" she said. "From the *Chronicle*?"

"Right!" The girl beamed over the fact that Constance knew her name. "It was no problem; I heard you on line before saying you wished they had them, so when I saw them bring out the tray, I figured I'd get you one," she said, lifting her shoulders. "I'll see you at the editorial meeting tomorrow!"

Lara scurried off and Constance laughed incredulously. "What was that?"

I smirked. "That was Billings clout at work."

Her entire face lit up. "Really? How cool! My first random perk!" She took a big bite of the croissant and smiled. I grinned in response, happy that she was getting the full Billings experience. At the beginning of the year it had seemed as if that might never happen for her. "Anyway, Whit is going to die when he hears about the Legacy," she whispered. "And Astrid and Lorna and Sabine! They're gonna be so psyched!"

I leaned back and took a sip of my coffee. "Actually, Sabine . . . not so much," I said bitterly.

"What? Why?" Constance asked, wide-eyed. Then her expression grew all-knowing. "Is it because she's foreign?"

I laughed, almost forcing the coffee out through my nose. Once again the Drake boys looked alarmed. As soon as the coughing fit subsided I was able to ask, "What's that supposed to mean?"

"Oh, just that she's not from here so she doesn't, like, know what the Legacy is all about," Constance replied.

"Ah." That actually made sense. But still, I was sure that wasn't the case. At least, not the whole case. "No. I don't know. She acted all annoyed that Noelle and I are working together on this."

"Oh," Constance said, nodding. "Yeah. That makes sense."

"What makes sense?" I asked.

"Just . . . well . . . don't take this the wrong way, but you have been spending kind of a lot of time with Noelle since she's been back."

"So?" I asked.

Constance lifted one shoulder and avoided eye contact as she shook another packet of sugar—her fifth—into her latte. "Just . . . maybe she's a little jealous." She glanced up at me as she stirred her coffee, then quickly looked away and took a sip.

"Oh."

Right. How had that not occurred to me? Sabine and I had been growing really close before Noelle returned. Constance was right. Jealousy made sense. But was she speaking for herself as well? By the pinkness of her cheeks and the sudden darting of her eyes, I had a feeling she was.

And maybe Josh, too

God. Was there anyone I hadn't been willing to ditch for Noelle lately? I thought of Josh, staring out at the cold Atlantic on a beach in Maine as his family reveled around a roaring bonfire in the background. Suddenly I wanted to be with him more than anything. When he got back, I had some kissing up to do. Big-time.

"Constance, I'm sorry," I said.

"For what?" she asked loudly.

"I've been—" I wanted to say *neglecting you*, but it sounded too egotistical. "Really busy lately," I finished. "But don't worry, I'm going to remedy that."

Constance grinned so brightly I was temporarily blinded. "Well, at least we'll all get to hang out together at the Legacy!"

That was my bright-side girl.

"Yeah. We will," I said proudly.

"And Whit! And Josh! Omigod. This is going to be sick!"

And Whit. And Josh. And Dash. Oh, my.

I was about to take another sip of my coffee, but pushed it away instead. The boy I'd used, the boy I was dating, and the boy I was flirting with behind everyone's back. Suddenly, all of us hanging out together started to feel a tad complicated. In fact, "sick" didn't even begin to cover it.

CREDIT

Sunday dawned crisp, clear, and cool—a perfect day for hanging out on the quad, admiring the changing leaves, and showing off new fall wardrobes. Led by our intrepid social chairs, the Billings Girls found a spot in the dead center of the action and staked our claim with cashmere Burberry throws. We settled in with all the books we weren't going to study and got right down to the real business of the hour: people-watching and gossiping.

"Can you believe Gage and Ivy are hooking up again?" Vienna said, unscrewing the top of a big silver thermos. She'd had several filled for us at Coffee Carma. "Isn't that sort of been-there-done-that? Get yourself some fresh meat already."

"Gage and Ivy?" Sabine gasped.

"How can you miss it?" Portia sneered, glancing across the quad. "They are all about the PDA."

We all turned to look. Sure enough, Gage was practically crawling on top of Ivy on the steps of Hell Hall. Tongues flashed. Her fingers gripped his sweater. His hands trailed under her skirt. I had to give them points for sheer idiocy. Didn't they know that any of dozens of teachers or administrators could trip over them at any moment?

"That's disgusting," Tiffany said, focusing her zoom lens on them nonetheless.

"Why her?" Sabine asked, clearly upset.

"Because she's got no standards," Noelle sniffed as she accepted a cup of coffee from Vienna.

"Don't let them bother you, Sabine," I said under my breath, squeezing her hand. Ever since my conversation with Constance the night before, I had been the perfectly attentive best friend. "I told you, you can do so much better."

Sabine smiled slightly, and turned her body so she'd have no chance of glimpsing the low-grade porn without sprouting a third eye. Good girl.

"Speaking of standards," Portia said, lifting her heavy hair over her shoulder. She was wearing an emerald green turtleneck sweater that, in the sunlight, brought out her eyes and made her dark hair pop. For the first time I could see why green was her signature color. "Is it true we're all going to the Legacy?"

"It's true," Noelle said, sipping her coffee.

"That's so incredible, you guys," Rose said, beaming. She smoothed her brown suede skirt under her legs as she adjusted her position on the blanket. "I've always hated the fact that we couldn't all go together."

"Well, now we can. If, of course, we can find out where it's being held," I reminded them. "Which reminds me, I have to make a call. Be right back."

I pushed myself up and walked a few paces over to a stone bench nearby. I had saved all of Jenna Korman's numbers in my iPhone, just in case, and wanted to put the last cog of our plan in motion sooner rather than later. I hit her cell phone number and sat on the cold bench while it rang.

"Reed Brennan! To what do I owe the pleasure?" her gravelly voice asked.

"Hi, Ms. . . . Jenna," I said. "Sorry to interrupt your Sunday."

"Not at all. Just golfing with my husband," she said brightly, then lowered her voice. "Boring as sin. Man couldn't beat me if Tiger was his caddy. So what can I do for you? You got the invitation, I understand?"

"Yes, thank you so much," I replied. "And we have almost everything we need."

A group of girls walking past my friends paused when they saw how close they had come to brushing by Noelle, then gave her a wider berth. I rolled my eyes. What did they think she was going to do? Bite their ankles?

"Good. Good to hear," she replied. "Walter! Bend your knees! You never bend your knees properly," she shouted off the phone. "Sorry about that," she told me. "You were saying?"

I stifled a laugh as the wind tossed my hair back from my face. "Well, all we need now is to get a copy of the last e-mail—the one that will reveal the time and place of the party. None of us are on the list, obviously."

"Not a problem. I'll have my daughter forward it right to you when she gets it," she replied.

I bit my lip. "Well, that's the thing. Apparently the Legacy planner is threatening to keep out anyone who helps Easton get in."

Jenna laughed wryly. "Well, good. The girl should learn to handle disappointment. She should have gone to Easton to begin with, instead of siding with her father. Lesson learned, I'd say."

My jaw dropped and I saw Noelle eyeing me quizzically. I couldn't believe that Billings was more important to this woman than her own flesh and blood. Maybe I still had something to learn about the significance of our house.

"Okay. Well, thank you," I said. "For everything."

"Not a problem. I hope we get to meet in person someday," Jenna replied. "Now if you'll excuse me, I need to go save my husband from another double bogey. Good-bye, Reed."

"'Bye."

Behind me, there was a commotion as Gage and Ivy got dragged off the steps by Mr. White, our resident disciplinarian. Gage was protesting loudly, but Ivy simply went along with a content-looking smirk on her face. Girl was such a freak.

"Well? What did she say?" Noelle asked as I strolled back to my friends.

Here was where Sabine would be proven wrong. I was the one who was really getting us into the Legacy. No one else could take credit for these phone calls with Jenna Korman. And everyone was here for me to deliver the good news. Credit, mine.

I was about to share when I saw Josh walking toward us across the quad, all fresh-faced and handsome in a white fisherman's sweater and cords, his overnight bag still slung over his shoulder. He looked at me almost uncertainly, and my heart gave a pang. It was all I needed to make a snap decision. The credit could wait.

"I'll tell you later," I said to Noelle.

"Reed. Come on! What did she say?" Noelle asked as everyone else grumbled.

But I didn't turn back. Josh waited for me as I skirted our picnic area and crossed the quad. Seconds later I was in his arms. As he held me, he let out a sigh that sounded a lot like relief. He smelled like salty air and firewood smoke.

"I'm sorry," I said over his shoulder.

"I missed you," he replied.

And then we went off to find someplace a little more private than the steps of Hell Hall.

GRATEFUL

The tokens arrived on Wednesday afternoon. I couldn't wait to hand them out, but considering Cromwell's anti-Legacy decree, we knew that the last thing we should do was open up a table in the cafeteria with a sign that read GET YOUR LEGACY TOKENS HERE! Instead we opted for a more secret locale. Just before the post office closed that evening, we delivered a stack of envelopes to the window, one for each Easton legacy, plus all the Billings Girls. We realized we could have just given them their rings in the house, but why should our friends miss out on the intrigue?

Then, Thursday evening after dinner, Noelle and I stole off to Gwendolyn Hall, hunkered down on the bench under the old, crumbling entryway, and waited. Gwendolyn was the original Easton class building—the oldest structure on campus along with the chapel—but it had been boarded up for years. All the windows and doors were covered with wooden planks and hand-painted KEEP OUT signs. Last spring I had asked Natasha why the administration hadn't torn it down, considering it was kind of an eyesore now, and she'd laughed at my naïveté. Apparently you didn't mess with tradition at Easton, even if it was covered in weeds and probably infested with critters.

"Check it out," Noelle said, pressing her finger into the wooden surface of the bench on which we sat.

I leaned over her knees to see which of the hundreds of etchings she was pointing at. There, carved into the wood grain, was a heart containing the initials DM + NL. It looked newer than most of the etchings, but definitely older than the freshest of the bunch. I forced myself to smile.

"When did you—"

"Dash did it. Freshman year," she said with a self-satisfied smile. "So not like him. Mr. Play by the Rules."

I wondered if it would surprise her to know that Mr. Play by the Rules had now almost kissed me twice, when clearly she believed that his heart belonged only to her. Of course, the moment I thought it, I felt guilty. Noelle was my friend. How could I have such traitorous thoughts while sitting right next to her?

"Ever come here with Josh?" Noelle asked.

"No," I said, the memories of Thomas that I always tried to keep at bay suddenly rushing in. "Not with Josh."

I looked away.

"Oh," Noelle said.

An uncomfortable silence fell over us. Thank God she spotted the first of our customers a moment later. Everyone had been given a specific time to show up, spaced at three-minute intervals. We had given Gage the earliest time, so we could get him in, out, and over with.

"Well," Gage said, grinning lasciviously as he climbed the steps. "This little scenario breeds all kinds of possibilities. Do you want to go one at a time or both at once? Because I'm down with either." He rubbed his hands together and practically licked his chops.

"Ew. Just stop," I said. I whipped out one of the small black boxes and handed it to him. Gage, who was apparently still entertaining the idea that his invitation to meet us here was some kind of sexual overture, looked confused. Until he cracked open the box.

"No way." He popped the money clip out, tossed it, and caught it. "Is this what I think it is?"

"You're going to the Legacy. Congratulations," I said, then looked at Noelle. "Although I'm now wondering why we included him."

Gage didn't seem to have heard me. He dropped to his knees and kowtowed at my feet. "I take back everything I ever said about you, Reed Brennan. Clearly you learned a few tricks back in the barn."

"Thanks. I think," I said.

Lance Reagan was the next to show. He glanced at me and Noelle and Gage, who was still on his knees, and looked a tad disconcerted. Maybe we shouldn't have chosen the most notorious make-out spot on campus for our transactions. But then, it was the number-one spot for a reason—it was private, hidden, and off the beaten trail.

"Dude! We're going to the Legacy!" Gage announced, jumping up and slinging his arm over Lance's wide shoulders.

"Seriously?" Lance asked, his eyes suddenly hungry behind his glasses.

"You can go now," Noelle said to Gage.

"What? Why? I want to play," Gage said, pouting.

"Because the whole point of this was to not draw a crowd and arouse suspicion," I said.

"Well, if you didn't want to *arouse* anything . . . ," Gage began, looking down at our legs, bare thanks to our skirts. I had dressed up for the occasion.

"Just go!" Noelle and I said at once.

Gage finally took the hint. Over the next hour Noelle and I handed out rings and money clips, enjoying the gushing gratefulness of our peers. Then, finally, Josh climbed the stairs. He was wearing a broken-in Harvard T-shirt under his houndstooth jacket and jeans with tiny holes in the knees. So cute my heart skipped a beat. I stood up and smiled as I handed him his money clip.

"Thanks," Josh said, not even opening the box.

"Aren't you going to open it?" I asked, disappointed.

"Oh, I know what it is. Gage is out there telling everyone."

Noelle and I rolled our eyes. "Unbelievable."

Noelle got up and trudged down the stairs to check on the situation. I was glad she had left us momentarily alone.

"Aren't you excited?" I asked, reaching for Josh's hand. "We're all going! Even me."

Josh smiled slightly. "Well, that part's good."

My heart thumped extra hard. Where were the thanks? Where was the pride over a job well done?

"What's wrong?" I asked.

"Nothing," he said, stashing the box in his pocket. "It's just . . . more drunken depravity? I think I'm kind of over it."

I felt like he'd just punched me in the gut. Here I was, running all over the place trying to get us into the Legacy—trying to save face for Easton and keep him and everyone else from missing out on the biggest party of the year—and he wasn't even going to thank me. Worse, he didn't even want to go. If Dash had been standing here, he would have been psyched. He would have thanked me for real. I was sure he would have.

God, what was wrong with me? I had to stop doing that. I had to stop comparing them.

"I'm sorry. That came out wrong," Josh said, holding my hand. "Of course we're going and of course it's going to be fun. And you should see how psyched everyone is out there. You've made a lot of people really happy, Reed."

Okay. That was slightly better. But I still wished that had been his first response.

"Idiots were all standing out there in a clump," Noelle said, reappearing. "Do they not get the point of the secret meetings? I swear, it's amazing any of them even got into this school."

She stormed by us and sat down again to consult our list of who was yet to come. Josh stepped closer to me.

"And I like that you're using your power for good instead of evil," he whispered in my ear. As he pulled back, his eyes darted to Noelle.

Message? Noelle was evil. So much for getting over it.

"Thanks," I said, rolling my eyes. And I forced a laugh. Because I knew he wanted me to take it as a joke, and I didn't feel like prolonging this.

"I'll see you guys," Josh said, acknowledging Noelle for the first time.

"Later, Hollis," she said.

As he loped off, I couldn't help feeling let down. Why couldn't he be proud of me? Why couldn't he support me? Why couldn't he just be positive for five seconds in a row?

SOME PEOPLE

That night I returned to my room after a grueling study session with Kiki and some other people from my AP chem class. We had our first major exam the next day, covering everything we'd learned so far this semester, and after listening to my classmates spout formulas and compounds and measurements, I was starting to think that I had, in fact, learned nothing. Maybe I could get Mr. Dramble to postpone the test. Did the Billings influence stretch that far?

Exhausted, I dropped down at my computer to check my e-mail. There was one from my brother, Scott, titled "Nittany Lions Rule!" That could wait. Another from my mom—a forwarded message, which was probably one of those stupid poem/chain letters that had been circulating the Web for years. Mom had just discovered e-mail, so all those urban legends and dumb-blonde jokes and stories of undying love we'd all read a thousand times were still new to her. I bypassed that as well and went right for the message at the top of the list. Sent only minutes ago.

From Dash. It was titled "Congratulations."

I glanced over my shoulder, as always, before clicking it open.

> Reed,
> I heard about your coup. Nice work! I knew you could do it. Whittaker is so excited I think he might have strained something. Is it too weird to say I'm proud of you? Is that something "just a friend" would say?
> WB
> Dash

So much better than that last e-mail. And see? This was the kind of response I had wanted from Josh. Pride. Congratulations. Was that so hard? My heart fluttered as I started to type a response, but then I paused, thinking of Noelle. Thinking of the fact that she and Dash were probably going to the Legacy together and that he—still— had neglected to tell me. I deleted the first line and started over.

> Dash,
> Thanks. And yes, I think just friends can be proud of each other. BTW, I heard you're going with Noelle. That's great.
> ☺
> Reed

There. That would show him how very unaffected I was by his— An e-mail popped up almost immediately. From Dash. He was online right now. Why did that thought make my pulse race like I'd just sprinted the four hundred?

> Reed,
> Yes. She told me she got one of the money clips for me.
> Good thing. There are certain people attending whom I'd like to see. . . .
> Dash

After that I couldn't stop smiling.

A PLAN

Our gowns were delivered the next day. All the other Billings Girls had received boxes from home or had ordered several dresses online so they could shop in the privacy of their own rooms. Even the ever-reluctant Sabine had received a gown from her mom. A gorgeous, modern white dress with a silk rope halter collar and an extremely low back. Everything was now in place, and everywhere we went, the Easton legacies were engaged in hushed conversation, speculating over where the party might be, who might or might not attend. The sense of anticipation was exhilarating. It put nearly everything else—classes, exams, Cheyenne, even Josh and Dash—out of mind.

But there was still one slight problem.

"I checked the fence on my morning run," Noelle whispered, slipping into the seat across from mine in the library. "It's sealed up."

"Damn. And with the security cameras on all the other entrances . . ."

"The Crom's really covered all his bases," Noelle muttered,

dropping her history tome on the table with a bang. "It's like we're living in Alcatraz."

"You're not giving up, are you?" I hissed, leaning over the table.

"Of course not," she snapped. "I'm just saying—"

We both looked up as a shadow fell across the table. It was Amberly, looking pert and perfectly matching as ever, with Lara and her other omnipresent friend hovering behind her.

"Hi, Noelle! Hi, Reed!" she said with a smile.

"Hi, Amberly," I replied.

I still didn't know what to make of this girl. She seemed sweet enough, but there was something blank behind her smiles.

"Omigod, Noelle, I just found out my family is going to be in New York for Christmas this year," Amberly said, clutching her books. "Now you can take me to all the good parties!"

Noelle smirked. "I would, Amberly, really, but my family always goes to the islands for Christmas."

Amberly's face fell like an anvil in one of those old Roadrunner cartoons. "Oh." And then it lit up again. "Well, maybe I can get them to switch their plans to the islands. My parents would do pretty much anything for me."

Good for you.

"I know. They're fabulous," Noelle said.

"What are *you* doing for Christmas, Reed?" Amberly asked me excitedly. "Are you going to the islands, too?"

I had to laugh. "Um, no."

"Well, maybe," Noelle said, eyeing me.

"Seriously?" I asked.

"Why not? You should absolutely come along. I'm sure Christmas in Blahtown, USA, is 'superfun,' but you haven't lived until you've spent the holidays in St. Bart's."

Okay. This was an unexpected turn of conversation. The very idea of living the sweet life with Noelle over break made my skin tingle. But could I really ditch the parentals and Scott for my mom's first sober Christmas in years?

"I'll have to think about it," I said. "But thanks, though."

"Oh, you have to come! Then we can all hang out together!" Amberly trilled. "I'm calling my mother right now." She whipped out a lime green phone, which perfectly matched the lime green stripe along the hem of her dark blue sweater, and flipped it open.

Noelle rolled her eyes as she shifted in her chair, turning to face Amberly's beaming face fully. "I don't mean to be rude, Amberly and . . . entourage," she said to the silent sentries standing behind her. "But we're kind of in the middle of something here."

Amberly hesitated for a second, then closed her phone. "What? What's going on?" she asked. "You can tell me, Noelle. We're such old friends."

"I know. We are," Noelle said smoothly. "But this is Billings business," she said. "Something you'll know all about in a couple if years, I'm sure."

Amberly lit up like the Fourth of July. Noelle had just thrown her the bone every girl at Easton wanted to chomp on. The possibility of getting into Billings one day. Behind her, her friends started to whisper urgently amongst themselves.

"Really?" Amberly said. Then, perhaps hearing how desperately grateful she sounded, she cleared her throat. "I mean, I'm sure," she added, lifting her chin a bit. "Well, if you need any help at all, you know where to find me. And don't forget to call me about St. Bart's! It will be so much fun! 'Bye, Noelle! 'Bye, Reed!"

She and her friends strolled away and I was about to launch back into our conversation when Noelle turned to me with her knowing smirk.

"You have a plan, don't you?" I said, recognizing that particular glint in her eyes.

"Not a plan, exactly," she replied. "But an inkling . . ."

Before I could ask her what she meant, I saw someone hovering just on the other side of the stacks behind Noelle. My heart skipped a startled beat. Someone was spying on us. Listening in. I saw a flash of blue eyes, white skin.

I jumped up, shoving my chair back.

"What? Reed? What's wrong?" Noelle asked,

I held up a hand and darted around the stacks. Irrationally, I thought of Cheyenne. I thought of Ariana. As impossible as either of those scenarios might be, someone was following me. Someone was watching. Who else? Who else would want to keep an eye on me?

I had no idea what I was going to say or do. No clue how I was going to confront who or whatever I was about to encounter. But in the next second I realized I didn't need to know.

Because no one was there.

THE REBEL

Saturday. October 30. Every secret exit from the Easton grounds had been checked. Every one of them was inaccessible. Short of a team of Navy SEALs busting onto campus and smuggling us out, we were screwed.

Noelle and I sat in the solarium that night, staring at each other across one of the smaller tables near the wall—a table a pair of sophomore girls had vacated for us the moment I started to eye it, saying they had been about to leave anyway. Everyone was watching us. Waiting for some direction. Some sign that we hadn't dangled the Legacy in front of them only to snatch it away at the last minute. But no one dared approach us. We were on lockdown.

"There has to be a way," Noelle said.

"We have to call Suzel," I whispered.

Noelle sighed. "I told you. I want to keep her out of this. We have to be able to do some things on our own."

"Noelle, the Legacy is tomorrow. Tomorrow. We still have to come up with a plan and tell everyone about it. There's no time left. And Suzel is not only on the board, but back in her day at Easton she was kind of a rebel."

I had read her file and, though it was next to impossible to imagine she of the straight teeth and responsible hair tearing up Easton, she had come close to expulsion a good six times in her first three years, engaging in everything from hazing to drug use to talking back to teachers. Then, her senior year, she had somehow become the model citizen she seemed to be today. What, exactly, had turned her around? That was the one detail the file didn't divulge.

Noelle, of course, didn't seem surprised by my revelation. She knew everything about everyone already.

"I'm willing to bet that she knows things about this campus that we can't even imagine," I said.

Noelle's eyes were serious as she studied me.

"The Legacy is tomorrow," I said.

She sighed through her nose. "Fine. Make the call."

I grabbed my iPhone and found Suzel's number on the contact list. She picked up on the first ring.

"Hello, Reed," she said in a bubbly tone. "How are you?"

"I'm fine, thanks. And you?" I said, sliding off my chair so I could pace out my nerves. I stuck to the wall so no one could hear my side of the conversation, but all around the room, people were noting my movement, pointing me out to their friends. It was like being in a cage at the zoo.

"I'm fine as well, thank you for asking!" she replied.

"Listen, Suzel, we actually have kind of a problem," I said.

"Shoot," she told me.

"Well, tomorrow's the Legacy and we still haven't figured out a way to get off campus," I told her, biting my lip.

Suzel sighed heavily, and for a moment I thought I'd messed up. That Noelle was right. That she was disappointed in us.

"I was afraid of this," she said. "Headmaster Cromwell is such a tightass. But you didn't hear that from me."

I laughed, both relieved and amused. Noelle's expression lightened considerably.

"All right. There is one passage off campus that he would never expect you to know about," Suzel said determinedly. "Get yourselves to Gwendolyn Hall tomorrow night at exactly six p.m. There's a wooden door in the back that leads to the basement. It's the only one they never boarded up. I'll make sure it's unlocked."

"Gwendolyn Hall?" I asked, glancing at Noelle. She eyed me, intrigued.

"Yes. There will be directions for you there," Suzel said. "And make sure everyone comes in shifts. A huge crowd is going to catch someone's eye. Understood?"

"Understood," I replied.

Her tone was so conspiratorial and no-nonsense, I half expected her to tell me that my phone was going to self-destruct at the end of this phone call. But instead, she just wished me luck and hung up.

"Gwendolyn Hall?" Noelle said. "That's miles from the gate."

"I know," I replied as I sat down again. "I told you. This woman's good." I took a deep breath and sighed. "There's still one problem."

"The Crom?" Noelle said.

"Yeah. He swore he was going to watch us all like a hawk," I said, running my hand through my hair. "I think we're going to need a distraction or something. Some way to keep him occupied while we all sneak out."

"My thoughts exactly," Noelle said with a sly smile. "And I have just the thing." She sat up straight in her chair. "Oh, Amberly?" she said in full voice.

Amberly nearly knocked over her chair, she jumped out of it so fast. "Yeah?"

The room was otherwise deathly silent. Everyone present was wondering why a non-Legacy freshman was being summoned by two Billings Girls.

"Come over here a second. And bring your little friends," Noelle said.

Amberly leaned down to whisper something to her girls and they all scurried to our sides like paid servants. I had no idea where this was going, but I liked it.

"Amberly, Reed and I have a little favor to ask of you," Noelle said, looking up at her.

The girl at least had the sense to appear skittish. "Sure," she said. "What kind of favor?"

"The kind of favor that will put the Billings Girls forever in your debt," Noelle said meaningfully, looking at each of the girls in turn.

All three of them turned beet red. They knew what this meant. Do this favor, and the Billings Girls will remember you. Do this favor and come junior year, you'll be invited to join the most exclusive house on campus.

"We'll do it," Amberly said. She didn't even need to consult the others. "Whatever you need."

Noelle smiled at me mischievously and I instantly knew what she was thinking. A distraction. Amberly's dorm was clear on the other side of campus from Gwendolyn Hall. If she could somehow summon Cromwell and the security guards to her dorm, we would all be free and clear. But the timing would have to be perfect, and the distraction would have to be realistic. There could be no chance of Cromwell seeing through it.

But of course, if there was one person capable of devising such a plan, it was Noelle.

"Good. That's exactly what we wanted to hear," Noelle said to the unsuspecting freshmen. "Now, here's the plan. . . ."

GWENDOLYN'S SECRET

Halloween night was frigidly cold. Our breath made steam clouds in the air as the sixteen Billings Girls stood, backs to the west wall of our house, and watched in silence as security guards flooded in from all corners of campus, racing toward Bradwell. I clutched the plastic bag that held my couture gown, my shoes, and my sparkling silver mask, chosen from a boxful of Legacy accessories Noelle had collected over the years. Aside from a few shouts, there was nothing but the sound of my friends' breathing.

"There goes Cromwell," Noelle whispered. Sure enough, the tall, hulking figure was slipping through the back door of the freshman and sophomore dorm. "Now's our chance."

I turned to the group, my pulse pounding through my temples, my wrists, my chest. "The first eight go now. The rest wait exactly three minutes, then run."

Everyone nodded.

"Okay. Let's go."

Sabine reached out and clutched my hand. We turned as a group and rushed toward the back of the dorm, then behind the trees toward Gwendolyn Hall, its crumbling edifice rising up against the starry sky like a haunted mansion. As we sprinted toward the back of the build-ing, every footstep sounded like a cannon shot, every breath like a whoosh of howling wind.

There was no way we could do this without getting caught. No way in hell.

I was the first to get to the back door, which was partially obscured by a century's worthy of ivy and weeds. I released Sabine's hand, said a silent prayer, and pushed at the door. It swung open with a creak that could have raised the dead.

"Let's go!" I whispered, ushering everyone inside.

As soon as the seven of them were through—Noelle, Sabine, London, Vienna, Tiffany, Rose, and Constance—a group of boys from Ketlar appeared, already dressed in their tuxedos. Josh gave me a quick kiss as he slipped by, and I ducked in after them, leaving the door open for the next wave.

"I don't like this," Sabine said, hovering just inside the entryway. "This feels wrong. It's spooky down here."

"It's okay," I told her, stepping into the freezing cold stone basement.

The ceiling was low—Tiffany, Noelle, Gage, Josh, and I had to duck—and there was a three-inch layer of dirt and grime on every surface. Dozens of ancient wooden desks were stacked and shoved haphazardly against the walls.

"I gotta go with Sabine on this one," Josh said. "Maybe we should just bag this idea."

I said nothing. I was not turning back now. As we stepped deeper into the room, squeaking and scurrying noises caused London and Vienna to yelp and clutch each other.

"Ew! Mice! I hate mice!" Constance cried.

Then she screamed at the top of her lungs. Gage had used his fingers to creepy-crawl across her shoulder.

"Constance! Shhh!" I whisper-shouted.

"Gage! Grow the fuck up," Noelle snapped.

The rest of the Billings Girls entered at that moment and the basement started to feel claustrophobic.

"What do we do now?" Tiffany asked.

"Directions. Suzel said she'd leave directions," I said.

Noelle and I and a few others spread out to look in the dim light pouring through high windows. The longer we looked, the harder my heart started to pound. What if she hadn't been able to get here? What if Cromwell had caught her? What if—

Then a lighter flared on. At that moment, I noticed a sweet, acrid scent filling the air.

"Who the hell is smoking in here?" Noelle blurted.

London and Vienna giggled. Several sophomores came in through the basement door.

Okay. Now I was pissed. Pot? As if breathing in here wasn't difficult enough already. "You guys! You're going to get us caught!"

London took a long hit on a skinny joint and passed it to Vienna.

"Sorry, Reed. We've smoked in every other building on campus, but we could never get in here."

"Gwendolyn's our holy grail," Vienna agreed, holding in her smoke, which made her face all flat and squinty. "We have now completed our toking tour of Easton!"

London and Vienna cheered, blowing smoke at the ceiling.

"Very mature," Noelle said, as Gage and a few others produced their own stashes from inner pockets. "Like you won't get enough of whatever you want at the Legacy."

"I think we're safe," Lance said, peeking out one of the low windows. "At least it doesn't look like anyone's coming."

"Guess Amberly's catfight was really convincing," Noelle said happily.

"I found something," Rose said. Suddenly a flashlight blazed in the dark. "It was over by the door."

At least someone was focused on the task at hand.

"Shine it around," I directed. She did as she was told, and I saw a flash of white. "There!"

Noelle and I lurched forward. Pinned to a warped wooden door that had been invisible in the darkness was a handwritten note.

> Girls,
> No one knows about this route other than the board
> and the school caretakers. And now you. Take the tunnel to
> the end. I'll have cars waiting for you there. Be safe.
> —Suzel

"Take the tunnel to the end?" Noelle repeated.

I reached for the side of the door and had to dig my nails into the rotting wood to get a grip on it. It took some effort to pry it open, and it kept getting caught on the stone floor. Finally Josh stepped forward to help me, and together we shoved it all the way back to the wall.

Rose shone the flashlight into the opening, revealing an impossibly tiny tunnel with dirt walls and floor. At the entrance were several more flashlights.

"She has got to be kidding," Noelle said.

Portia put her hand to her chest as she peaked in and grimaced. "L.O.T.I."

"Huh?"

"Laughing on the inside," Rose clarified Portia's abbreviation.

"What the hell is this, the underground railroad?" Gage asked, blowing pot smoke right in my face.

"I'm not going down there," London added. "No way."

"You guys, Suzel would not have sent us here if it was dangerous," I told them, grabbing one of the flashlights. "We have to go before someone notices the lights. If you're in, follow me. If not, just make sure you're not seen sneaking back."

"Wow. That was very authoritative of you, Reed," Noelle said, without a hint of teasing.

"Thanks," I replied, ducking through the entryway.

Josh grabbed my wrist, stopping me. "Are you sure about this?"

I glanced over my shoulder at him. My heart was pounding, and my palms were sweating so badly the plastic bag around my gown was slipping from my grasp. But all those faces were looking to me expectantly. I wasn't about to back down. Not after all that work. I wouldn't let everyone down.

"I'm sure," I said.

I handed him the flashlight and took his free hand in mine. There. That was much better.

"Now let's go."

MY MOMENT

The tunnel let out through the side of a hill, smack in the middle of the woods. Josh and I gulped the fresh air as we emerged. I felt like we'd been feeling our way along the passage for hours, but when I glanced at my watch, I found it had been only a fifteen-minute walk.

"Now what?" Josh asked, as the others crowded out behind us.

We moved the flashlights along the tree line. It was pitch-black.

"There!" I shouted, ecstatic to have spotted a pathway through the trees.

Josh and I forged ahead with Sabine, Constance, Noelle, and Gage at our heels, the others trailing behind. Two minutes later, we found ourselves at the side of a quiet road, where a line of stretch limousines awaited our arrival.

At the sight of the cars, the entire Legacy crowd hooted and hollered. Several people slapped me on the back, hugged me, kissed me.

I think that, until that moment, many of them had their doubts that I was going to pull this off.

"Reed, you are going to go down in Billings history," Tiffany said, snapping my picture.

"Try Easton history," Lance added.

"Reed Brennan, you are a goddess among girls," Gage told me.

"Gage, you just said something to me without insulting me in the process," I said.

"Must be the pot." He laughed and strolled toward the cars.

"This is your moment, Reed. Savor it," Noelle whispered in my ear as she slipped by me. And so I did. All these people were happy and laughing and excited because of me. Because I had refused to give up. I couldn't have stopped smiling if I even wanted to. It really was my moment.

"You gonna put that on?" Josh asked, looping his arm around my waist as he looked down at my still-bagged gown.

All around us, girls were disrobing right in plain sight and slipping into their dresses.

"I'll be right back."

I ducked back into the trees to do my own quick-change. Josh followed after me.

"Why, Mr. Hollis. Think you're going to sneak a peek?" I joked, glancing at him over my shoulder.

He blushed and scratched at the back of his head. "Well, no. Unless, of course, you want to give me a peek."

Josh had never seen me naked. I had never seen him naked. In a towel, yes, but not fully naked. But right then, in all the revelry and adrenaline of the moment, I was feeling brazen. Daring. It was Legacy night. The night anything could happen.

And so, there in the middle of the woods with his flashlight shining on me, I stripped slowly down to my underwear, never taking my eyes off his. Josh watched my every move. I felt less self-conscious in front of him than I had felt in front of Noelle and Darla the seamstress. I felt like I wanted him to see me. I thought he would fidget or blush, but he was mesmerized. He looked at me like I was the most beautiful sight he'd ever seen.

Then I reached back and unhooked my bra. That woke him up.

"What are you—"

"My dress is strapless," I told him.

"Don't." He stepped forward and picked up my gown, unzipping the bag around it so fast I thought he was going to tear something. He lifted the dress out and held it up to my half-naked body. "Someone could come back here. I don't want anyone to see you—"

His eyes were pleading and I instantly understood. He didn't want anyone to see me but him. I loved him so much at that moment, I wanted to cry. So what if he didn't care about the Legacy? He cared about me. He loved me.

"Okay, not now," I said. Then I leaned forward, the dress between us, and kissed him. "But soon?"

Josh swallowed hard. I could tell it was taking everything he had to control himself. "Soon. Definitely soon."

Suddenly, I couldn't have cared less that Dash was going to be there tonight. In fact, I now intended to avoid him completely if at all possible. All I wanted was Josh. All I needed was Josh.

"Maybe we should just stay behind tonight," Josh suggested, his voice thick. "Just you and me."

There was a second there when I almost said yes. Who wants to turn down a proposition like that? But then someone on the street shouted, and I laughed. "Josh, we can't. It's the Legacy."

Something shifted in his eyes as he looked at me. For a second I thought he was going to start in again. About how unnecessary this whole thing was. How lame. I braced myself. Felt my adrenaline start to rise. My defenses snap into place. But then he smiled.

"You're right. It's the Legacy," he said. "So get dressed already and let's go."

Thank God. I wasn't sure I could deal with another speech right now. But I suddenly felt shaky. Like I'd just come very close to some steep precipice. Like tonight had just been rendered fragile. I shoved my feet into my dress, and tried not to think about it.

Five minutes later we were all settled into our limousines and I was nestled in between Josh and Sabine. Noelle, Constance, Gage, Tiffany, and Rose made up the rest of our party, while everyone else had crowded into the limos behind ours. There were champagne bottles chilling on ice in the bar, but no one had cracked them. No one spoke.

We all stared at my iPhone and waited. And waited. Dead silence.

I looked at Noelle. It was almost seven o'clock. This could not be happening. After everything we'd been through, we could not be foiled because Jenna Korman's daughter didn't want to send us a text.

And then the phone beeped.

I grabbed it up, heart in my throat, and elation overcame me. "We have the address!"

"What is it?" Rose asked.

"It's 2325 Bayshore Drive, Boston."

Josh, Constance, Tiffany, even Sabine whooped happily. But over it all, Gage and Noelle spoke in unison.

"No effing way."

My heart dropped at their tones. His angry. Hers incredulous. "What?"

Rose looked like she'd just swallowed a worm.

"What?"

Noelle reached over and grabbed my phone from me, staring down at it.

"That's Ivy Slade's address."

OBLITERATED

"This place is sick," Josh said, practically pressing his nose to the window. He hadn't spoken much on the three-hour drive, so I was gratified to hear him say something so positive. One thing I loved about Josh in general—he was so not jaded. Even with family homes in New York, Berlin, Paris, Maine, Vail, and Hawaii, he was always still able to see the opulence and beauty in his surroundings.

No one else seemed at all fazed by the modern mansion that rose before us as the limousine pulled up the winding drive, but I had never seen anything like it in my life. Set into the side of a rocky cliff over-looking Boston Harbor, the house was white, with at least five floors, each with floor-to-ceiling windows that stretched all the way around the square façade. Outdoor decks circled each level—the lowest being the widest—and they all overflowed with revelers. Up on the roof, more Legacies gazed down, holding drinks and curiously watching the arrivals. The decks had been decorated with colorful flags in orange, red, and gold, which whipped around in the frenzied breeze. Between the altitude and the wind coming off the water, it seemed like a wind-swept locale.

Our car pulled up in front of a massive smoked-glass door. Outside stood two guys who looked like they'd just gone AWOL from the Marine Corps. They stared us down as we toppled out of the car, giddy with triumph and champagne.

"Ladies," the taller and darker of the two said, stepping in front of the door. "Gentlemen," he added with a sneer, as Gage cackled at one of Lance's jokes. He'd been getting messier and gigglier with every swig of alcohol. "You have something to show us?"

"Sure do!" I trilled, stepping forward and holding out my hand.

The guy checked out my ring. There was a brief moment of total silence in which I was sure he was going to spot it as a fake—that Ungari had somehow outed us by making our Ls too big or using the wrong gold or something—but then he nodded to his buddy, who turned and opened the door. I twirled by him, laughing with relief. God, I wished Ivy had been there just then, watching as we so easily crashed her party. Every time I thought about her smug face, about the fact that she'd spent the past few weeks strolling around campus, believing she'd outwitted us, it made me want to throw something. I couldn't believe she had tried to keep her own classmates out. Including the guy to whom she was currently giving up the goods in front of the entire school on a daily basis. She must have worn a wig to order the invites and tokens, thinking a disguise and a bad alias would be enough to hide her secret. What, exactly, was her inner malfunction?

If she hated Easton and everyone there so much, why the hell had she come back?

But no matter. We had the last laugh. I could not wait to see her face when I finally did find her.

I hung by the door until my friends made it past the Legacy police. Once Josh and all the Billings Girls were through, I stepped inside.

The center hall stretched to the sky, open to all five floors. High above, connecting the east side of the third floor to the west, was a catwalk about four feet wide, with chrome guardrails on either side. Directly above that, in the center of the high ceiling, was a perfectly flat, square skylight, which afforded a stunning view of the stars above. Toward the back of the huge hall two spiral staircases stood, stretching, up, up, up into the house, all the way to the roof. Everything was black and white, except for the red marble floor beneath our feet, the framed modern artwork on the walls, and the incredible multicolored modern sculpture—all twisted metal and sharp angles—directly in the center of the room. Around it, waiters and waitresses delivered iridescent cocktails to the couture-clad girls and tuxedoed guys. Laughter and chatting filled the well-lit room. For now it was all very civilized. The real Legacy had yet to begin.

"This is unlike anything I could have possibly imagined," Sabine said, sufficiently awed.

She hadn't seen anything yet. But why spoil the surprise?

"I hate to say I told you so—"

"But you were right. I have a feeling this is going to be a night I'll never forget," Sabine said earnestly. "Thank you, Reed."

I grinned. Better late than never.

As we moved further into the wide-open center hall, deep, melodious bells chimed all over the house, echoing loudly throughout the room. Signaled by the chiming, all the guests poured in from the outdoor decks, and the noise level grew to a deafening pitch. Somewhere nearby, Constance squealed. I turned and saw her throwing herself into Whittaker's arms, the skirt of her green gown kicked up so high I got a glimpse of a purple thong.

Constance wore thongs. Shocking. I turned away, not because of her creamy white butt cheeks, but because I was sure that if Whit was there, Dash couldn't be far behind. And I wasn't ready for that. Not by a long shot.

The bells all went silent at once. The guests looked around in curious anticipation. There was a distinct sizzle in the air.

"What's this?" Sabine asked.

"The welcome," Noelle said, sidling up to join us. She tilted her head toward the sky, and there was Ivy Slade, striding out onto the catwalk above our heads. She wore a black-and-white striped gown with a sweeping train and a variegated hem, each stripe trailing out a bit longer than the last. Covering her eyes was a huge black feather mask, the plumes of which stretched at least two feet above her head on the right side. Her face was pale, her lips a deep red. She looked like something right out of the pages of *Vogue*.

From behind her back, she lifted a large silver bell and shook it. The chime echoed throughout the house. Everyone fell silent.

"Welcome one, welcome all!" Ivy called out, looking imperiously around the room. "It is my honor to host this year's Legacy and to welcome you all into the inner sanctum. Of course, this year, the inner sanctum is all around us."

She opened her arms wide to encompass the entire house.

"On each floor you will find myriad pleasures to tickle your senses," she continued, striding along the catwalk as she looked down on us all. "So come. Enjoy. Immerse yourself. And remember . . . what you see here . . . what you do here . . . who you touch here . . . who you screw here . . ."

She paused, slyly eyeing the now laughing crowd.

"*All* will remain here," she said. "For this is the Legacy, my friends. You are the chosen."

"Yeah, but chosen by whom?" Noelle muttered.

"So make peace now with whomever you worship and never . . . look . . . back!"

All the lights in the house were doused. There was a general gasp, a momentary panic, and then thousands of moving strobes flicked on, accompanied by a driving dance beat, flooding the room with an insane whirl of color. The cheer was intense. The dancing began instantly. People shouted. Hands grasped. Drinks were poured. In all the mayhem I almost lost sight of Ivy, but she was coming our way. Descending the steps. Holding her gown up with both hands as she nodded to her guests like she was the queen and they mere peasants. Before she could even hit the floor, I was shoving through the crowd.

"Reed!" Josh shouted. "Where are you—"

"I'll be right back!" I replied.

Through sheer force of will, and major bicep strength, I arrived at the foot of the spiral staircase at the exact same moment as Ivy.

"Ivy Slade!" I shouted.

A screeching girl in a hot pink gown ran by me, driving her heel into my foot as she was pursued by some guy who had already lost his shirt. I barely even noticed the pain. Ivy looked at me quizzically.

"Yes?"

I whipped off my mask. Her reaction was filmworthy. Her jaw dropped. Her skin grew waxen. And then, shock over, a steel veil descended over her eyes.

"Who let you in?" she said through her teeth, swooping toward me like a black-and-white bat.

I lifted my hand. Under the lights, my gold Legacy ring flashed red, then pink, then green, then yellow. Ivy was hypnotized.

"Amanda Hold?" I said, savoring the total shock on her face. "And thanks ever so much for inviting *all* of Billings," I added, putting on a sickly sweet voice. "How very generous of you. I'm sure we're all going to have just the most fun!"

And then, satisfied that I had obliterated her big night, just as she had tried to obliterate Easton's, I backed away with a smile and melted into the crowd.

THE CHOICE

Hours passed. Or maybe it was minutes. I wasn't sure. I was drunk. It was all sweat and bass and bodies and hands and silk and skin and blur. I hadn't seen Josh in forever. Not since I'd left him to find Ivy. But I hadn't moved. Not really. I'd spent the whole night on the same floor, dancing with whatever configuration of friends was there at any given moment. I didn't need to visit the druggie floor. Didn't want to visit the sexy floor unless I first found Josh. So why move? Why not just drink and dance and sweat? If Josh wanted to find me, he could find me.

Why didn't he want to find me?

"Reed! Here!"

My vision blurred as I spun around, and I held my head until it passed. Okay. That was weird. Perhaps I should slow down on the alcohol intake. When my sight finally cleared, Sabine appeared before me, holding out a frothy pink drink. Three, actually. One for me, one for herself, and one for Vienna. She was having a good time. I could tell. Her forehead shone with sweat and her eyes were bright. Because she wanted to check out every inch of the party, she'd been getting drinks for all of us all night and exploring as she went. The Legacy had officially won her over.

"This party is unbelievable!" she shouted, pushing her straw around as some girl dragged a guy off the dance floor, his hand already working down the top of her dress.

"I know! This is exactly what I needed!" I replied. Then hiccupped. Then laughed. My brain felt like it was bobbing happily on a river of pink froth. "Isn't it fabulous to just not have to think?"

Sabine smiled. "Absolutely."

Just then, a pair of arms encircled my waist. I was about to throw them off—random guys had been attempting to grope me all night—but then I felt Josh's familiar, soft lips on my neck.

"Hey!" I cheered, turning around in his arms. A bit of my drink sloshed over onto his sleeve. My vision blurred again and I had to grasp him to keep from falling sideways. How much alcohol was in those pink things, anyway? "Where've you been?"

"Around," Josh said. He leaned right into my ear, so I could hear him without him yelling. "Hey. You wanna get out of here?"

Something stirred deep, deep down below. I smiled. "Like, up to the roof?"

Word had traveled fast that there were several tents set up on the roof, for those more modest partiers who didn't want to grind with each other in a group setting—which was apparently what was going on up on floor three. I so didn't want to know.

Josh's expression darkened a bit. I blinked. What happened?

"No. I mean, like, get out of here. Go. Head home," he said.

I stepped back unsteadily, and his arms fell away. He had to be kidding me. We'd just gotten there! Hadn't we?

"Really? You want to leave?" I asked.

"Who wants to leave?" Vienna shouted, slinging her arms around me. Her purple dress had slipped so low there was definite visible nipplage. "You can't leave! No one's even hurled yet! My money's on Constance. She's such a lightweight and—"

"Not now, Vienna," I said, throwing her off.

"Fine. Buzzkill," she griped, dancing away.

Josh's hands were in his pockets now. "I just . . . I'm not into this, I'm sorry. It's the same as it is every other year and I'm just . . . bored. Can't we go somewhere and be alone?"

He said this in a leading way and my mind flashed back to the woods. To my half-naked self. To him suggesting we bag the Legacy and stay home and, it was implied, have sex. Him and me. Our first time. He wanted it to be tonight.

But why? Why now? Why tonight? Was it simply because he didn't want to be here? Was he trying to find the one thing he could dangle in front of me to make me actually leave with him?

It was so manipulative. So . . . passive-aggressive. So . . . not Josh. And something inside of me snapped.

"Why tonight?" I demanded. "We can *be alone* practically every other night of the year! Why do you have to do this now?"

Josh's eyes flashed. "I thought . . . I mean, *you* said 'soon,' remember? I thought . . ." He looked at the ground, frustrated. Some big, thumb-headed guy careened into his side and Josh shoved him away without a glance. "Or is drowning in Fuzzy Navels suddenly more important?"

"No! I meant it. I meant *soon*," I replied as I dodged another pair of lethal high heels. The bumping, grinding, raucous atmosphere was not making this conversation easier. Neither was the fact that my head was starting to pound in time with the beat of the music. I was having a hard time focusing on Josh's face. I took a deep breath and concentrated. "Just . . . not now. Why do you want to make me leave? You knew how much I wanted to be here tonight. You knew—"

"And *you* knew I *didn't* want to come here, but I did. Now all I'm asking you to do is leave a little early. To be with me. You'd think you'd want to be with me, considering you're supposed to be my girlfriend. Considering, I don't know, we're supposed to be in love!" The thumb-head slammed into him again, laughing as he moshed with his friends. "Get a life!" Josh shouted, shoving him once more. The guy laughed and loped off. Thumb-head was not helping the situation.

"Josh, I do love you," I shouted blearily. "You know I do! But why do I have to prove it by leaving here? Do you have any idea how much work I put in just to get us here? I don't want to leave yet. I'm having fun!"

"This is fun? *This* is fun!?" Josh shouted back. "A bunch of drunken idiots pawing each other and acting like it's some kind of privilege? I thought you were above all this, Reed! I thought you were better than this!"

"Better than this? This is *your* world, Josh. I'm just trying to be a part of it," I snapped. "God! When did you get to be such a downer?"

Josh clenched his jaw and looked at me, hurt. "When did you get to be such a Billings Girl?"

The way he bit out those final two words, he may as well have said "bitch." I felt like he'd just dug my heart out with a shovel. Tears welled up in my eyes, but I refused to let them spill over.

"Screw you," I said.

Josh stared at me. For a moment I thought he was going to walk away, but he didn't. "I'm sick of this, Reed. This isn't you—blowing off your friends, getting trashed, acting like you're above everyone."

My jaw dropped. "I do not act like I'm above everyone!"

"I don't like what these people are doing to you, and I can't just stand by and watch it happen. I'm sick of it. It's time for you to choose, Reed," he said, stepping closer to me. "It's them or me."

I glanced at my friends, but it took me a good couple of seconds to find them. They'd moved their dancing selves a few feet away, ostensibly to avoid the argument. Noelle laughed as she tossed her hair back. Tiffany twirled Portia under her arm. Kiki attempted to instill some form of rhythm in Constance. They were having fun. Like they were supposed to be. And I . . . I was miserable.

"I just wanted to have a good time tonight," I told Josh, feeling weak and rubbery all over. "I love you, but I want to have a life. I shouldn't have to choose."

"Well, I'm asking you to," he said.

This was not happening. He was not forcing me to do this. He was not forcing me to break up with him. Forcing *me* to say the words, when he was the one making everything so damn difficult. It wasn't fair. It just wasn't fair.

"I can't do this," I said, backing away from him. My head shook from side to side of its own volition, swimming in fizzy pink drinks. "I can't."

He stared at me. The resignation on his face was clear. "Then I have to go. Have fun with your *friends.*"

There was such venom in the word. Such anger in his eyes. When had Josh become so mean? So judgmental? How could he say he loved me, then look at me that way? And how could he so easily just turn his back and leave?

The crowd swallowed him. I suddenly became aware of the music again. It was everywhere. Around me, inside me, forcing its way through me.

Had he just broken up with me? Was that what had just happened here?

Someone elbowed me in the face. I was hip-checked into a curvy chick's backside. On this dance floor if you didn't keep moving, it was your funeral. The entire room spun and spun and spun. Suddenly, I had to get out. I needed air. I needed to think. I needed, quite possibly, to puke. Looked like Vienna's bet on Constance as the first hurler was going to be a bust.

"Reed! Reed!"

Sabine shoved her way over to me. I hadn't even realized she had gone.

"Sorry. I have to get out of here," I said, clutching her arms for balance.

"Wait. Here! Someone gave this to me and told me to give it to you!" she announced, excited. She wrested one arm from my fingers and held up a folded piece of paper like it was the golden ticket.

"Who?" I asked, trying hard to breathe evenly.

Had Josh and I just broken up? Had we?

"I don't know! Some girl. She wore a mask like everyone else," she said, clasping her hands. She was really loving the mysterious aspect of the Legacy. "Open it!"

I did. The letters were fuzzy, and I had to squint to make out the message. It read, quite simply, "Meet me on the roof."

"Oooh. Intrigue!" Sabine said with a gasp. "Are you going to go?

The room whirled before me again. What girl would want to meet me alone? And why did it have to be the roof of all places? After last fall, I wasn't a fan of heights in general, especially not roofs. I pressed my hand to my forehead. My body heat was starting to skyrocket. Just like it always did right before I heaved.

Okay. So maybe some fresh air was a good idea.

"Yeah. I'm going to go," I said.

And before I could vomit on Sabine's brand-new shoes, I fled.

GONE

I stumbled along the lollipop-colored bungalows on the roof. The air was cool and crisp. I could breathe again. I could think. And everything was becoming clear. Perfectly, sharply clear.

Josh and I had just broken up. He'd made me choose. In his mind I had chosen the Billings Girls. He'd left me here. Left me. How could he do this to me?

Someone inside one of the bungalows laughed and I snapped to, remembering why I was there. A glance around revealed a few couples standing near the guardrail, looking out at the view. Some guy was sucking on some girl's neck, sitting on the edging around the skylight. Otherwise, there was no one. No single girls waiting for me. I looked at the note again.

Meet me on the roof.

It was not a girl's handwriting. Not at all.

My heart started to pound. What was going on here? A few staggering steps. Two feet away from me, a girl moaned in ecstasy. A champagne cork popped. Someone shrieked. I turned around, lost my balance, and a hand grabbed my arm.

I didn't even have time to resist. The hand pulled me into a red bungalow. Pulled me against a warm, firm body.

"What are you—"

The eyes were deep. Warm. Brown. He took off his black mask. My mouth watered. It was Dash.

"You're here," I heard myself say. My brain felt buoyant. Unfocused. My limbs weak.

"I've been watching you all night." His hands ran across my bare shoulders as his eyes moved over me. My face, my hair my shoulders, my breasts, my hips, and back to my eyes. "I couldn't take it anymore; I had to touch you."

"Dash—"

It was barely a gasp. My constricted lungs wouldn't allow anything more. His eyes were so intense. So searching. Was he on something? Considering where we were, it was more than likely. But I couldn't tell. Maybe I was too drunk. Maybe, right then, I didn't care. All I knew was that there was too much air between us. Too much space. It was mere inches, but it was too much.

"Reed, I can't . . . You're all I think about. I can't do this anymore. I can't. Please. Please . . ."

I found myself stepping closer to him. There was no way I could stop. This was bad. This was very, very bad. But we were alone. And this was Dash McCafferty. Strong. Handsome. Impossibly sexy. And Josh . . .

Josh had left me. He'd left me here all alone. My heart hurt so much all I wanted to do was forget. To lose myself. Lose myself in this.

"Please . . ."

He was begging. Begging me to touch him. Dash McCafferty. Begging me.

This was the Legacy. Anything could happen. And no one. Would ever. Know.

"What do you want to do, Dash?" I whispered.

And then he kissed me.

Everything inside of me exploded. I instantly weakened and sank into him. He held on to me, his strong arms around my back, and held me up. Held me to him. Pressed every inch of his body into every inch of mine.

God, what had we been waiting for? How could we have let this go for so long? If I had known that kissing him would feel like this—would make my entire body vibrate with pleasure—I would have kissed him at the Driscoll. I would have kissed him at the Vineyard. I would have kissed him last year at any and every chance I had.

Dash pulled me forward. He was shaking. And I knew. He felt it the same way I did. Our bodies needed to be together. Needed to feel each other. Needed to ride this psychotic rush wherever it took us. He backed toward the silk-draped mattress. I didn't resist in the slightest.

When he pulled away from me, I fell forward a bit, my lips searching for his.

"What—"

He smiled. Then he swooped me up in his arms like a child. The feathers on my skirt tickled my skin, and even that was somehow arousing. As Dash laid me back on the bed, I grabbed his jacket and pulled him down on top of me. I just wanted to feel his weight. Feel his body. Feel every inch of him.

"God. Could you be any more gorgeous?" he whispered, trailing kisses down my neck.

I reached behind his head and pulled his lips down on mine again. From there, it got very heavy, very fast. My dress was loosened. His jacket was off. My breast was exposed. His shirt was unbuttoned. I watched my fingers as they worked the closure on his pants, hardly daring to believe what I was doing. But I couldn't stop. Couldn't. Couldn't. Couldn't. I needed him. Now.

Dash's fingers slowly, tremblingly, moved up my torso toward my chest. I sighed in ecstasy. Somewhere outside, someone shouted. There was a crash. Breaking glass. A cry. I barely even noticed. Didn't notice a thing other than Dash's body, moving fully on top of mine.

And then, the curtains were flung open. And Josh was there. And all the hurt and betrayal and anger and shock and pain in the world was reflected in his eyes.

"Josh!"

And then he was gone.

OVER

What. The hell. Was I doing?

I shoved Dash off me, yanked up the zipper on my gown, and almost fell over in the process. Righting myself, I shoved my way out of the tent. Dash shouted something after me, but I couldn't even comprehend it. The roof and all the colors spun around and around as I searched for Josh.

No. No. No.

My heart felt like someone was jamming an ice pick into it over and over and over again. My stomach lurched. I heaved for breath. It was no good. I turned around and all my insides came out through my mouth. All over the pristine glass of the skylight.

"Ew! Bitch!"

"Nasty!"

I dragged my hand across my mouth. Tears poured from my eyes. I couldn't be this drunk. I tried to think back and count the pink drinks. There had only been three, maybe. Maybe four. Or was it five? On a full stomach. And yet I couldn't focus. Couldn't stop my mind from whirling. Could barely even stand up straight. What was wrong with me?

Then I heard someone shout and, holding my hands to my head, I looked up. Josh was just shoving his way past a group of revelers through the door, into the house. I wasn't too late.

"Josh! Josh, wait!"

I stumbled forward, tripping on my feathers, and yanked up my skirt, balling it in one hand so I could sprint. Down a few steps to the fifth floor. Tripping. Gripping the guardrail. Everything spinning. Everything a blur. There were people everywhere—passed out against walls, sucking face on the floor, talking and drinking and smoking. It was all distorted. All wrong. But somehow I saw Josh fling himself down the spiral staircase at a run. Bumping along the hallway from one side to the other, I attempted to follow.

The moment I started down the spiral stairs, my stomach heaved again. I looked down, and four floors of partiers stretched and contracted and turned below me. Some unsuspecting dancer was going to get thrown up on. I turned inward, covered my mouth, and kept running. Luckily, Josh got off at the fourth floor. I stumbled off the last step and managed to take in a shaky breath. I got a mouthful of pot smoke—there was a huge group of kids on the floor violating all manner of bongs—but somehow I still felt better. I lurched forward and grabbed his arm.

"Josh, please. Please! We need to talk!" I cried.

He turned around and looked at me. There was nothing but pity and disgust in his eyes. I reached for him, but he backed away. I had to press my hands into the wall to keep from falling over.

"You're a mess," he snapped.

"I know. But Josh. I didn't . . . I didn't know. . . ."

What was I supposed to say? How could I possibly explain? I was so confused. So hot. So desperate. I just wanted him to stop looking at me that way. I just wanted him to look at me the way he had in the woods. The way he had when he first told me he loved me. I wanted to go back. I had to go back.

"I came back here to apologize," Josh said stonily. "I came back here to tell you I felt bad about what I said. That I felt guilty. But where do I find you? I find you half naked, pinned under one of my best friends!"

He shouted this last part so loudly I flinched, and several of the bong Buddhas around us laughed.

"Dude, chill. It *is* the Legacy," one of them said.

"Josh, please. I didn't know what I was doing. Something's wrong with me. I feel . . . I didn't—"

"Think you were going to get caught?" he spat. "Well, you did. And just so we're clear, we're over. As of right now, I don't ever want to see you again. Good-bye, Reed."

He turned around, shoved some guy aside, and ran.

"Josh!" The tears flowed like a waterfall now as I stumbled after him. "Josh, no! Please! You can't—"

But he was too fast for my addled self this time. He hit the staircase and disappeared.

"Omigod. Omigod. Omigod." I was hyperventilating. There was no air. I pressed my face into the cool wall and let my whole body follow. Josh was gone. Really and truly gone.

And all around me, people were laughing. People were talking and shouting and shoving and smoking and dancing and kissing and touching and drinking. And Josh was gone. Really and truly gone.

I had never felt anything like the pain in my chest, in my stomach, in my lungs. And suddenly, I knew that I couldn't survive without him. I closed my eyes. All I wanted to do was close out the pain. Sink to the floor and stay there for the rest of my life.

And then, someone laughed. My eyes popped open as an icy chill chased down my spine. I knew that laugh. That was Cheyenne's laugh.

Someone brushed by me. I forced myself to turn around. Once again, my vision blurred, but this time I was prepared for it. I closed my eyes, took a deep breath, and opened them again. And there she was. It was her. Picking her way down the hall of stoners with three other girls. Laughing. Her hair. Her smile. Her figure. Her chin beneath the pink sequined mask. She wore a gauzy white gown with a pink sash. Pink. Cheyenne's favorite color. Her hand was on another girl's back as they navigated along. In two seconds they'd be gone.

I forgot about Josh. I had to. For that moment he ceased to matter. I had to find out what the hell was going on. Was Cheyenne alive? Was I insane? Hallucinating? Hearing things? No. I couldn't be. She was right there. My head pounded. I couldn't think straight. But I had to know. I had to know for sure.

"Wait! Cheyenne! Wait!" I shouted.

They didn't stop. Didn't look back.

"No! Wait! Come back!"

I followed after them. Tripped on someone's outstretched leg. Braced my hand against the guardrail. Her laughter floated back to me. Even as the hallway turned beneath my feet, I kept moving.

"Cheyenne! Wait! Why are you doing this? Please, just stop!"

Through the haze of smoke and sweat and heat, I saw Cheyenne hug one of her friends, then duck into one of the rooms down the hall. Perfect. She was alone. She couldn't get away now. Working on pure adrenaline, I shoved aside a pair of giggling girls, kneed some guy in a George W. mask in the balls when he tried to grab me, and lurched for the door.

My heart pounded in my throat as I slipped inside, turned, and closed the door. I waited for my brain to stop turning in my skull and took a breath. I was petrified to turn around. Irrational fears flooded my mind and brought out goose bumps all over my skin. Fears of vengeful spirits and specters and zombies and death. I was petrified to turn around. But I did.

And the room was empty.

BFF?

I really was losing my mind. There were no other doors at this end of the hallway. I could have sworn she had come through here. And yet . . . nothing.

That was when I really started to cry. I groped my way to the queen-size bed in the center of the room, convulsing, clutching my stomach, choking for air. I cried like I'd never cried for Cheyenne. Like I'd never really cried for Thomas. Something even bigger had died tonight. My heart. My love. My future.

Selfish, I know, but true. And when I realized this, I curled into a ball and cried some more, now thinking of those people I had lost. Thinking of the total uselessness of their deaths. Thinking of how I'd have given anything to have them back.

For the past few weeks I had distracted myself with tasks. With the presidency, with the Legacy, even with school and Dash. But there was nothing here to distract me now. Nothing but this empty room. And the weight of it all pressing down on me.

I don't know how long I stayed like that, curled up on the deep red comforter, tearing and snotting all over some stranger's bed. But after a while, the sobs subsided. I realized I was exhausted. All I wanted was a tissue, some aspirin, and to curl up here and wait for morning.

Pushing myself up, I glanced around for the first time. There was a cabinet next to the bed with a lamp and several issues of *Paper* and *Nylon* stacked on top. No tissues. I crouched down and opened the doors, and out slid three photo albums, one of which fell open at my feet.

My heart seized up. There, right in the center of the page, was a glossy five-by-seven photo of Ivy Slade and Cheyenne Martin.

They were young. Maybe thirteen. Cheyenne had braces. Ivy, glasses. They were both beautiful. Adorable and fresh-faced and grinning. Their arms were flung around each other's shoulders and each held a tennis racket in her free hand. A handwritten caption underneath read, "Cheyenne and Ivy, Doubles Champs!"

My throat was so dry I started to cough. Dropping back on my butt, I looked around the room. The wall directly across from me was a collage. The entire wall was covered with words and images. Some clipped from magazines, some printed on photo paper, some on flimsy newsprint. They were partial images. Lips, but not faces. Petals, but not flowers. Wings, but not birds. Clouds, but not sky. Still, it wasn't the jarring disconnect of the images that made me stop cold. It was the word, painted in red script against the black wall in the center of the collage, that stopped me.

The word *IVY*.

This was Ivy's room. I was in Ivy's room. And Ivy had pictures of Cheyenne.

My hand shaking, I turned the page. There were several, smaller photos on this one, but Cheyenne and Ivy were a major theme. I turned the pages. On every one, images of the two girls greeted me. Cheyenne older, no braces now, clinging to the bow of a boat. Ivy and Cheyenne, maybe fourteen or fifteen, trying out water skis. Ivy and Cheyenne in formal attire, full-body hugging with their legs kicked up in back. The two of them on horses, on the beach, standing in front of Bradwell.

"Me and Che at the Regatta"

"Ivy + Cheyenne = BFFs"

"Me and Che, first day at Easton!"

Ivy and Cheyenne, Ivy and Cheyenne, Ivy and Cheyenne.

This didn't make any sense. Cheyenne and Ivy hated each other. Cheyenne had all but spit when Rose and Portia had suggested we offer Ivy an invite to Billings. And Ivy detested all of us, but especially Cheyenne. She sneered whenever the girl's name was brought up. But now, suddenly, I was finding out they were BFFs?

I slammed the album closed, shaking now with anger. More lies. Everything was lies. Everything was secrets. It was just like last year, when perfect Thomas had turned out to be a drug dealer, and sweet Ariana had turned out to be a lovesick murderer, and Natasha had been secretly dating Leanne Shore, and Taylor had disappeared in the middle of the night, with no explanation, never to return. This world was nothing but rewritten histories. It was all about what you could get away with. Who you could deceive. Had anyone been honest with me ever? Was it some kind of Easton law that people couldn't tell the truth? Was there a secret course being given in deception that I didn't know about?

Instantly, Josh's devastated face came back full force and I laughed ruefully. Way to be a hypocrite, Reed. I didn't need a course in deception. What the hell had I been doing since the beginning of the year? Flirting with Dash. Lying to Josh. Lying to Noelle. I was just as bad as the rest of them. Josh was right. I had become one of *them*.

I shoved the books back into the cabinet and stood up. This was it. I was done. No more lies. I was going to find Noelle and tell her what had happened with Dash. I was going to tell her I had feelings for him, no matter how muddled and confused those feelings were. I was going to 'fess up and take whatever was coming to me. Noelle was going to go ballistic, I was sure, but at that moment I didn't care.

I was sick of the lies. And I was going to do something about it.

THE GOOD NEWS

"Noelle! Noelle!"

She was gabbing with some girl I'd never seen before. Tall and willowy, with red hair and a distinctly regal air. As I raced toward her, Noelle nearly spit out a mouthful of her green apple martini.

"Reed! What happened to you? You look like shit," she said.

The willowy girl flicked her eyes over me like I'd just rolled in off one of the fishing boats in the harbor. She quickly, silently moved away.

"I know," I said, trying to ignore the warning siren going off in my head. The siren screaming at me that this was a bad plan. A bad idea. That if I told the truth I was a dead woman. But it didn't matter. I didn't matter. All that mattered was the truth. "Listen, I have to talk to you. Like, now."

I gripped both her arms and pulled her toward the wall.

"My God, Reed. What's the matter?" she asked me, her brown eyes concerned.

"I—"

"Wait! Good news first!" she announced. She took a sip from her drink and placed it on a nearby table.

"You have good news?" I said weakly. Bonus. Maybe her good news would defray the sting of my weapon of mass destruction.

"The best," she said, grasping my hand. "Dash and I got back together!"

And so the world stopped turning.

0 FOR 2

When? When? *When?*

For the rest of the night that one word kept repeating itself in my mind.

Sitting on a chaise waiting for my friends to finish up with their debauchery . . .

When?

Clutching my bare skin against the frigid air as our limo made its way to the head of the line of a thousand limos . . .

When?

Sitting on the velvet limo seat with Gage's head in my lap while Noelle and Portia applied lipstick and mascara and bronzer to his drooling face . . .

When?

When had Noelle and Dash gotten back together? Was it before he grabbed me, before he kissed me, before he felt me up and pinned me down and helped me shatter Josh's heart? Or after?

Which was worse?

If it had been before, then he was an asshole. An asshole who was using me and cheating on his girlfriend. If it was after, then why? Did he decide he didn't want to be with me? Had my body repulsed him back into her arms? Or did he think I didn't want to be with him, because I'd gone after Josh? Had he meant to go back to her all along and was just waiting until after he had his way with me?

I was going to be sick again. Only this time I was going to be sick all over Gage's unsuspecting face.

"Reed, smile!"

I looked up. Noelle was holding Gage's clown face up in my lap as Tiffany wielded her camera. The flash blinded me. Everyone laughed. I turned to stare out the window, and at the purple spots floating before my eyes.

"I've never been kissed like that in my life," Sabine gushed to Constance. "And I never even got to see his face! Do all American boys kiss like that?"

"Lay one on Gage and find out!" Noelle joked.

More laughter. They were still having fun. Still buzzed. Still high. The Legacy had been a success. For them.

But I . . . I had lost my boyfriend and my potential boyfriend, all in one night.

Zero for 2 on Legacy outcomes for me.

Next year I was staying home.

WORTH IT

The tunnel seemed tighter on the way back to campus. Tighter and colder and devoid of air. Like when you take a trip and it takes no time to get where you're going, but forever to get home. I just wanted out of there, and so it seemed it would never end. And then it happened.

Up ahead, someone started coughing. Seemingly at the same time, smoke filled my lungs. And not pot smoke this time, but real smoke. Thick and black and suffocating.

"Turn around! You guys! Turn around!" someone shouted.

There was a scream. I turned around. Constance, who had been in front of me, but was now behind, was shoved into my back. I tripped and fell into Vienna, who hit the floor. It was a stampede. Mayhem. My pulse pounded in every vein as panic took over. We were all dead. We were all going to get crushed and suffocate and die.

"Stop!" Noelle shouted at the top of her lungs. She was a few people behind me now. She had been leading the way. "Everybody calm down!" she said in her authoritative tone. Nobody moved. "Now pick yourselves up."

I helped Vienna to her feet in front of me. The smoke was getting thicker now. Vienna was crying.

"Now cover your nose and mouth with something and walk. Walk fast, but walk," Noelle said. "We're not that far from the opening."

And so we walked. I gripped my feathered skirt to my mouth and tried to breathe. Vienna grasped my hand with her sweaty fingers behind her, but she kept moving. Someone in the tunnel was whispering a prayer over and over again. I supposed when the privileged were trashed *and* scared, they got religious.

Soon the smoke started to thin, and the vibe calmed considerably. When I finally found myself back out in the fresh air, I was almost numb with relief.

"What was that?" Tiffany asked as Portia and Noelle, the last of the group, emerged from the tunnel. Their faces were streaked with black, and Portia bent over in a coughing fit. Rose stepped forward to help her. Clearly they had gotten the worst of it.

"I don't know," Noelle said. "But we're going to have to walk back and go in the front gate."

A sort of grim resignation settled upon the group. This was it. We were going to go through the gate, with its guard and its cameras, and we were done for. I looked around at all of them, and hoped it had all been worth it.

For me, it definitely had not.

MY CURSE

The guard let us in. He was not surprised to see us. He simply nodded, buzzed the gate open, and watched as we trudged through, our couture dirty and soot-stained and ragged. The walk up the hill was excruciating. Not only did those of us who were less trashed have to help drag the semiconscious along the steep road, but we all dreaded reaching the top. Who knew what we would find? Who knew whether we'd be instantly expelled? And how bad was the fire? Had people been hurt? And—my own personal torture—where was Josh? Had he tried to get back that way? Was he okay? Would he ever want to see me again?

As we finally reached the first dormitory circle, the sky was turning a nice, rosy pink. We wouldn't even have the cloak of night now so that we could sneak back to our dorms and delay the inevitable. We were beyond dead.

And then we all saw it at once. The black plume of smoke rising above the trees.

"It's Gwendolyn Hall," Rose said grimly.

We knew this. Of course we knew this. But someone had to say it.

"Let's go," Noelle ordered.

Together, we all walked around Bradwell and came into the quad. No one even tried to hide or hang back or sneak off. The guard had us all on tape. Might as well stick together.

Unlike with all the other tragedies I had experienced on campus, there was no crowd of students this time. Only teachers, firemen, cops, and EMTs. The students, clearly, had been ordered to stay in their rooms, but their faces were visible in every window, pressed to the glass, staring down at us.

Four fire trucks were parked around what remained of Gwendolyn Hall. They had cut ugly, jagged turrets in the grass and kicked up dirt and mud all over the pathways and lawns. One hose still poured water over the smoking remains. Blackened stones were strewn everywhere. Crumbled mortar, singed trees, broken glass. A mountain of busted rock. Gwendolyn Hall, the original Easton class building, the oldest edifice on campus, was no more.

We had done this. This was our fault. Who lights up in the basement of an ancient building with hundreds of aged wooden desks pushed against the walls? Those things were kindling. A conflagration waiting to happen. One match left behind. One smoldering joint. That was all it took.

We had brought down Gwendolyn Hall.

A few police officers moved aside and I saw Headmaster Cromwell, dressed in a full suit and tie, nodding gravely as one of the firemen spoke to him.

What had we done? What had I done?

"We should probably get out of here," Lance said.

He was right. No one had even noticed us standing there yet. But right then, as if Lance's whisper could have carried all the way across to Cromwell's ears, the headmaster lifted his head and looked right at us. His expression was one of unadulterated ire, and I felt it to my very core.

"He knows," Gage said, still drunk and therefore stating the obvious. "Oh crap, he knows."

Instinctively, I looked at Noelle. She was still. Grim, but still. And every other person in our dingy, bedraggled crew was looking at me. Stepping back. Leaving a good, safe circumference around me. That's when I knew for certain. This was on me. It was all on me.

I should have seen it. Should have known all along. The blessing of the Billings presidency was nothing but a curse.

Look out for the next instalment
in the *Private* series

AMBITION

BY KATE BRIAN

The higher you climb, the further you have to fall . . .

The school administration is threatening to close the
exclusive Billings Hall for good and, as president, it's up to
Reed to save her beloved home. So what better way to
win over the headmaster than to host a glamorous
fund-raising event in New York City?

But rumours and suspicion are rife, and the police
are asking questions about the mysterious death of
Cheyenne Martin last year. Someone wants to see
Billings – and Reed – go down. And they'll
stop at nothing to make it happen . . .

Coming soon . . .

The PRIVATE series
KATE BRIAN

Welcome to Easton Academy, where secrets and lies
are all part of the curriculum . . . but these secrets
must be kept private whatever the cost.

Set in a world of exclusive boarding schools, Kate
Brian's compelling *Private* series combines the bitchy
snobbery of the elite and wealthy, with secrets,
mystery and satire. Dark, sinister and sexy
– with no parents around to spoil the fun . . .